CHATTERBOXES

A Collection of Urban Microfiction
Volume-1

By
Kevin M. Scott

DEDICATION

To the ones who show up without showing off—

who cheer from the shadows, check in without agenda,
and love me without needing credit.

You remind me that family isn't always blood, and blood
isn't always family.

This book is for you.

Acknowledgments

First and foremost, I thank GOD for the gifts He placed in me—my passion, my purpose, and the strength to keep walking in both. Every page of this book exists because of His grace AND mercy.

To my parents: your unwavering love, support, and belief in me have carried me farther than you will ever know. You built the foundation I stand on.

To my sister, **PABLO**—my constant encourager and number one fan—thank you for reminding me, again and again, that I was meant to finish this. Your voice has been a lifeline on the days when doubt tried to win.

There are countless others who deserve recognition, and I know I will inevitably miss someone who played a meaningful role in this journey. Please know that your impact is woven into these pages even if your name isn't written here.

But there are a few HEROES I must honor directly: **Dorothy Cooper, Barbara Hill, Mrs. Guadalupe, Jack Bossard, Virginia Carson, and Mrs. Ellis**—thank you for seeing something in me long before I fully saw it in myself. Your guidance shaped my path in ways I'm still discovering.

And to the man who changed *everything* for me—**Gary Andres**. You called my mother and begged her to let me join your journalism class, and that single act altered the entire trajectory of my life. I wish I had the chance to say "thank you" to you one more time. REST IN POWER!

To all of you—named and unnamed—thank you. This work is as much yours as it is mine.

Peace and Blessings!

Kevin

Thekevinmscott.com

TABLE OF CONTENTS

JADE, MIA & BRYSON

Jade? Girl, is that you?

In the flesh. How are you doing, Mia?

Damn, you're not supposed to look that good after having a baby.

Thanks; after I had this little guy, things changed, not just physically, but that's what everyone sees.

You look fabulous in that dress.

Thank you.

And this little chocolate kiss is the cutest thing. I want to hold him when he wakes up.

Sure. He's a good baby.

He's so cute. Are you in town visiting?

No, I moved back.

What? And you can't call anybody?

I didn't know I was going to make this move until Friday. It took a lot of decision-making and consideration, but we're here.

Did you tell Irma you were moving back? Or Pam? She's going to freak out.

Nobody yet. It was indeed a last-minute decision. Closer to family and his dad, you know?

Absolutely. Those are the best decisions. Life is too short to wonder and think about what's next.

Yeah, you have to do what's best for your family.

Well, I know everyone will be excited to see you and Little Mister Hershey Chocolate… so cute!

Thanks.

And I'm here for you anytime while you get adjusted.

About that, can we go somewhere and talk? Safeway's yogurt section differs from where I imagined having this conversation.

Sure, sure, girl. How about you come to the house? I'll whip something up, and we can catch up.

That sounds good.

Ooh. How bout I call the girls over and surprise them? Bryson will be home at eight, but he'll be excited to see you, too.

So eight o'clock?

No, come before that. Bryson will be home at eight, maybe later. If that isn't too late for you and the baby?

Oh no, not at all. I feed him around that time. He'll be out like a light for a while.

Aw, he's so adorable. Bryson and I decided to wait until the firm makes him a partner before we start making babies, you know?

Mmm hmm.

We wanted to be solid in our careers first, and things took off quickly for us both.

Mmm hmm.

Is something wrong?

I'm going to go, Mia. I'll see you in a few hours.

Perfect, I'll whip up something for us.

Ok.

By the way, Jade, what's your baby's name?

Bryson.

DAVE'S DIFFERENT

Did you talk to Dave about Saturday?

Me?

Yes, You.

If Dave doesn't know women aren't feeling his bohemian look, I don't know what to tell him.

He prefers Vintage.

Veronica prefers not to be seen around him.

So you called Veronica?

Dave is crazy about her.

What did Veronica say?

She'll come, but she wants to bring Vicky.

So they want to mooch.

Veronica isn't comfortable around Dave anymore.

But she'll order everything off the menu.

That only happened once.

Twice, if you count Vicky.

I don't believe their parents can tell them apart.

That shit wasn't cool.

You're mad because they fooled you, too.

This isn't about me. Dave wants people to like him for him.

That's why he dresses this way?

Yes.

To prove a point?

Exactly. To prove a point.

Why doesn't he just find a grungy girl downtown?

He's not a perv.

They're of age. They're attending Art College.

Not his flow.

How long will this phase go on?

You mean, when will we get the old Dave back?

Yes! Remember LA?

I remember.

We couldn't go anywhere with Bible man.

Bible man?

C'mon, man! He doesn't wear real clothes anymore.

It's Dave.

I get it. I think I get it. I mean, it hasn't changed us.

Oh, it's changed us.

You know what I mean.

Hey, it is his money.

True.

Please don't get Veronica to do your dirty work.

What do you mean?

She's his weakness.

It's manipulation.

She's a woman who switches places with her twin sister.

We like who we like.

Right, but if he ever reveals he's loaded, she'll love him.

No one knows he won the lottery except me, you, and God.

What do you want me to do?

Talk to Dave about Saturday.

FIRST DATE

This place hasn't changed in 20 years.

If it ain't broke.

Right.

What made you pick this place?

Do you remember the first time coming here?'

Yeah, it was Martina's 25th birthday. We turnt up.

No, silly, I'm talking about the first time *we* came here.

Aww, how could I forget? It was my birthday too.

You ordered shrimp and grits.

No, you ordered shrimp and grits. I wanted chicken and waffles.

Really?

Really.

After all these years, I don't think I knew that.

Yep. I love shrimp and grits more than chicken and waffles now.

How come you didn't say anything?

Because I liked that you ordered for me.

But you could've said something.

I only wanted to say, 'Check, please.'

Wait, you didn't enjoy yourself?

Of course, I did.

So why did you want to bounce?

I wanted to bounce on you.

Oh really?

Really.

Check, please!

THE CLIENT

Carolyn Mims.

Hi Carolyn, it's Sasha, Sasha Monroe. Sasha Hardy, but hey.

Sasha Hardy? Oh my goodness, it's been forever.

It has.

How are you, girl?

Uh, preggers for the third time, but I love being a mom.

Aww, that's sweet. Do you know what you're having?

Another boy. My daughter is officially outnumbered now.

Well, she's got you to overrule anything.

Speaking of which, I'm starting my own firm.

Whaaaaaat?" That's amazing! You go, Sash—Black Girl Magic at its finest.

That's what's up. Congratulations. For real.

Silvia Wooden says you're at Downs, Ford, and Stratton.

Yeah. It is no big thing.

A lawyer at DF&S? I beg to differ.

A token black lawyer and a sistah. I check the boxes.

You do more than that, I'm sure.

I get the softball cases, but it pays for Cancun and Maui.

I'd like you to work for me.

Excuse me? Girl, for real?' I'm flattered.

I will pay you what DF&S pays you, plus 22 percent.

Stop playing.

And no softball cases. Your offer letter is two minutes away.

Sasha, I don't know what to say.

Say, 'Yes.' I need people I can trust.

Right.

I can trust you, right, C?

Duh, of course. That's a silly question.

There's nothing like having your own on your team.

Of course, Hey, that's the door.

It's the courier with your offer. He'll wait for you to sign it.

Sure.

Are you there?

I'm here. I'm just skimming through things before I sign this.

Right. Did you sign it?

Signing right now, and the courier is handing me my copy.

Perfect.

I'm excited, and the start date is 30 days from Monday.

Ted will counter, but he's receiving a buy-out letter.

Dang, Sasha. You are about your business. I'm impressed.

Thank you. Your first case will be to represent me.

You?

Yes, in my divorce.

Wha-what?

Earl's been cheating on me.

What? Wait? Earl Hardy?

Yes, for quite some time. Do you know Earl?

Oh, Sasha, I'm sorry. And with the baby and everything.

We'll be fine, and you'll mitigate the case and make it amicable. Right.

Right?

Of course.

Good.

Sasha, why don't I come over so we can talk about all of this?

No. Stay there and make room in your closet for Earl's things.

What?

Goodbye, Carolyn.

Hello? Hello? Sasha? Sasha? Sasha! Shit!!

NEW GIG

Are you nervous?

Meh. I've had jobs before.

But this is in another country.

I work with these people all the time.

But you're in their time zone now.

I call that convenience.

Another set of rules.

I'm doing the same gig, so to speak.

But everything is different from the US.

Just new faces here and there, but it's nothing to worry about.

Maybe I'm just excited for you.

And I'm excited you came with me.

What better way to burn my vacation time?

We didn't talk about that before we left.

I tried, but you slept most of the flight.

I've never been horizontal on a plane.

The beauty of first class.

That part.

How long do you want me to stay?

I'll be head-down for a couple of weeks, adjusting.

And?

And we won't be able to spend a lot of time together.

I know what I signed up for.

I'm just saying I have extra responsibilities, so…

So, I'll go sightseeing during the day, and you can tell me about yours at night.

And you figured this out when?

When you were knocked out in your pod.

It was likely the wine.

I had champagne

Check you out.

Plus, my sister told me where all the good stores are here.

Don't spend it all in one day.

Trust me; I know how to shop, even in the UK.

I've always wanted a classic suit.

I'll look for one of those bespoke shops.

Excellent. Although no one dresses up anymore.

They do here. That's why you're going to love it.

And what happens when your vacation account zeroes out?

You let me worry about that, Mr. International.

That has a nice ring to it.

You deserve it. You've worked hard for this promotion.

And what better way to say 'Dueces' to the haters?

Oh, you're going to encounter them here, too.

And I thought you were the optimistic one in this relationship.

You're a brother transferring here to run the show.

Tia, I've worked with all of these people before.

I know, but it was over Zoom. You're their boss now.

I don't see it that way.

Ok. You know how some of them feel about Americans.

I'll be alright.

You'd better, or I will send for them.

Dang, honey. It's going to be alright.

I know, but you'll be flying solo once I leave.

So, first, let's fix the pouty face.

I'm not pouting.

Next, look at the view. Beautiful right?

Yes, it is incredible.

After I officially check in, I have Friday and the weekend off, so let's sightsee and shop.

I'll be here and ready when you are.

SH*T SHOW

Yo! You good?

Thanks for scooping me, man.

I'd never thought I'd have to bail you out of anything. Daphuq?

Let me cashzap you right now.

Fahgeddabodit. Talk about how you got here in the first place.

I lost my cool at this art exhibit.

Dayum. Was the art that bad?

Nah, man, Joy's dude tried to flex on me.

Daphuq? You and Joy a thing again?

Pfft. I'm keeping it a buck with you.

Please do.

I saw her from across the room and waved. That's all.

Joy is still digging you, Bro.

I didn't even expect to see her at this event, Fam.

You turned her on to this world, and she's all cultured now.

Whatever. At that point, she was probably on Moscato number four when she stepped to me.

Aw, sheeeet.

And her dude steps as well and tries to flex.

He's either blind or more giant than you, which would be rare.

Nah, but Joy had too much to drink and was being her sassy French self, moving like Shakira.

Aw, sheeet.

Yeah, the dude just walked up to me and pushed me.

So why am I bailing you out and not him?

Because I knocked his ass out.

For real?

Gave him a chop behind his ear.

One blow?

That's all it takes if you know what you're doing.

And you do know what you're doing.

Exactly!

What did Joy do?

She started making a scene, cussing in French, Portuguese, or both.

Feisty and fine

I have to admit, she's feisty.

And a troublemaker.

Yep, feisty and not as refined as when she was with me.

She likely lost a bit of the culture you instilled in her.

I saw that eye roll. Po-Po was there in two minutes flat.

It took that long, huh?

They were cool—this time.

Of course. You can't shoot a brother in a multimillion-dollar art gallery.

Now that would have been one hell of an exhibit.

A Sh*T Show!

FAMILY

Have you got everything?

Everything I have is out of that big trunk of yours.

You left your backpack in the back seat.

Appreciate ya cuz. I knew you had my back.

Fa'Sho.

If I left anything, it would give me an excuse to fly right back.

I'm here.

Yeah, I love it out here too. I'm coming back.

Word.

The weather, the women, the vibe. It's all good.

I'm glad everything aligned with your visit schedule.

Last night's party was lit, and on a Monday too?

It goes down like that out here, cuz.

I gotta come back. I'm glad I came to see you, fam.

Me too. Tell everyone I'll be back for Turkey Day.

Cool. Well, give me some love before this long-ass flight.

Don't come back for Thanksgiving.

Pardon me.

You heard me.

Why? Is everything alright?

Our family's fucked up, and you're doing too good out here.

What? You're buggin'.

Aunt Phyllis will probably ask you for a loan or something.

Big Momma would kill me if I didn't come home.

Yeah, the message *was* from Big Momma.

Get the hell outta here.

Swear, cuz. She told me to tell you right before I left.

Damn, yo.

Yeah, bro. It's real, and she cares too much about you.

I love her to death as well. Why would she say that?

Tell you what. I'll come back and see *you* for Turkey Day."

"A'ight. That'll work, I guess.

Peace.

Peace. Hey, Cuz! What if you bring Big Momma out to see me?

When was the last time you saw Big Momma on a plane?

I can't recall.

She doesn't even like bridges.

You're right.

Peace, cuz. I'mma get on this bird. I'll see you in November.

Bet.

GROOMING

What are you doing?

I got a hair bump or something.

Down there?

Well, I've got hair down there, so, yes, down there.

How did that happen?

I'm not a hair bump expert.

What did you think you did to get it?

I don't know what I did, dear.

Were you running, working out, or wearing tight undies?

All of the above, your honor.

I'm serious.

Me too. I've been running, lifting, and wearing Spandex.

It never happens to me, and I take kickboxing twice a week.

I also have more hair.

Where?

Down there.

I get the landing strip special.

And I appreciate that strip.

I'm going to take you to see LuLu.

That's a hard no.

Men get tidy down there nowadays, and I bet you LuLu will say: *No Hair Bumps, no More.*

LuLu will say more than that.

Nasty.

SOLICITUDE

Are you OK?

Would it matter if I wasn't?

Yes, that's why I asked.

I'm not OK.

Well, what's the matter? Spit it out.

It's not something I can just spit out

Of course, you can. Just say it.

Nah. We've been on a nice streak of sex for the last eight days.

What's that got to do with anything?

I'd prefer to keep the streak going.

But, still, something's not OK, though?"

Nope!

So, do you want to discuss it or not?

Not.

Doesn't seem fair, especially if you're going to have an attitude.

It's my issue, and there's no attitude.

Seems like it.

You're not responsible for my happiness or attitude.

With that attitude, I sense our streak is about to end.

No attitude. I need to clear my head, so I'm going for a run.

A run? A run will help?
Yep. See ya in a few.
OK.
OK.
But you're not OK.
I'll be OK after my run.

OLD FRIENDS

Gerald Tanui's office.

Yes, hi, I'd like to speak to Gerald. Thanks.

To whom may I say is calling?

To whom? That's fancy. Tell him it's Jeff Young.

Are you able to hold, sir?

Yep. Holding.

Thank you for holding. Are you a client of Mr. Tanui or Mr. Young?

Client? I'm his boy.

Excuse me?

We played ball together.

Oh, that's nice. Is there something Mr. Tanui can help you with?

He can help me by speaking with me.

Is this related to a legal matter, Mr. Young?

Yes, it is. Basically.

Are you able to hold, sir?

Yep. Holding.

Hold for Mr. Tanui, Mr. Young.

That's what's up.

Jeff?

Gerald? What's up, my guy? It's Jeff from P.S. 22.

Right. Long time, my man. How can I help you?

Aw, man, it's good to hear your voice.

Likewise, Jeff. What's on your mind?

Man, do you remember that shot you made?

What shot, Jeff?

Against Langston High, G! The buzzer-beater?

Jeff, that was years ago, man. I hardly remember.

Not me, bro.

Oh yeah?

I'm the one who passed the rock to you.

That's right.

Like Grant Hill to Christian Laettner.

It's not that epic, but I get it.

You were on the local news and in the papers, man.

Pretty big for teenagers.

Yep. Coach Moore started calling more plays for you.

Meh.

And you got more coverage on TV.

Not more than anyone else, Jeff.

Dunno, man. If you don't make that shot, you don't get calls.

I always thought it was Randy Hess' team, if you ask me. Played for Boeheim at Syracuse.

Yeah, but you were a hooper too, man.

Meh. Do you remember Matty? I wonder what he's up to?

Matt Sanders played at SMU. Nice jump hook.

That was a long time ago, Jeff.

You've had some helluva games for Yosemite State.

Thanks.

You're welcome.

So what can I do for you, Jeff? I only have a few minutes.

I think you owe me some scratch.

I beg your pardon.

You don't go to Yosemite if you didn't make that buzzer-beater.

Are you serious right now?

Like a heart attack.

Jeff, that was one pass, one shot in one game long ago.

But you got more shots after that shot.

Hmmm. Interesting perspective, Jeff.

It is.

What do I owe you for that assist, brother?

You're the fancy lawyer. What's the rate for that?

What will satisfy you, Jeff?

Two hunnid.

Two hundred dollars?

Make it three. Yep, three hunnid.

That's it?

Yeah, man. That's it.

Marina won't tell me you're on the line asking for more?

Nah.

OK.

OK.

Is there anything else I can do for you, Jeff? I have to go.

I just wanted to call you and talk about that shot you made.

Hold the line. I'll send you back to Marina.

What does she look like, G?

I appreciate the call, Jeff.

It's good to hear from you, too, G. Stay in touch.

SCHEME

Dang. It's raining.

Again.

I know. Pouring.

Do you want to cancel?

I kinda want to.

Are you serious?

I am.

This is going to be the 4th time we have rescheduled.

It is the first time because of the rain.

People aren't going to come at all if we reschedule again.

Strategy.

Are you implying you don't want company?

I simply mentioned the rain.

You and your moods.

I'm more temperamental than moody, but it is raining.

If we reschedule due to the rain -

If we reschedule due to the rain, people will understand

You're right. It's raining. We have to reschedule.

Exactly.

They're going to know it's you.

Me?

Yes. We rescheduled because of you.

I made it rain?

You probably willed it to rain.

You give me too much credit. I did no such thing.

Who did I marry, Storm?

I got powers, but not like this.

Well, since it's raining, show me whatcha working with.

Do you want thunder or lightning?

Give me both!

Strip!

PRIVILEGED

I wish you wouldn't do that.

It was just two dollars.

But you're giving them a reason to continue standing there.

It was two dollars.

They can go find a job and make thousands of dollars.

I'm sure, but for now, he's getting my dollar.

He's going to remember our car.

I doubt that.

They could be buying drugs.

With two dollars?

All he needs is five or ten to score.

Listen to yourself.

I'm serious,

Do you know the druggie protocol?

You know what I mean. He'll collect enough to buy drugs.

Or be here long enough to pay for the shelter.

What?

There's an entry fee to shower, eat, and wash clothes.

I didn't know they had to pay to stay at a shelter.

The shelter has bills, too. The homeless aren't paying the bills.

But I thought it was all grant-funded

The grants fund the food, buy supplies, or pay the bills.

Here.
A twenty?
Hurry before the light changes.
God bless you.
But ask for your two dollars back
Incredible.

LESSONS

Where are we going again?

A food bank.

Because?

A few reasons.

Can you give me one or two of these reasons?

Sure. It's the right thing to do.

That sounds like a mission statement.

What do you know about mission statements?

I'm just saying. Sounds wonky.

Ha - Using one of your mom's words.

Mom uses a lot of wonky words.

That, she does.

This is a sense of giving back to the community as well.

Giving back?

Yes, we feed over 2500 families in less than 3 hours.

Filling boxes?

Filling boxes.

Wow. What is another reason we're going to this shelter?

We're going to a food bank, not a shelter.

And why are we going again?

The main reason?

Yes, not the mission statement reason.

How about what happened at school?

So this is a punishment?

It's not a punishment, but I want you to know that other people have more significant issues in life.

She called me the N-word, Dad.

So.

So? She said it like she'd said it before.

And choking her unconscious was the answer.

I bet she won't use that word anymore.

It's not your job to choke out everyone who uses that word.

You weren't there, Dad.

You're right. I wasn't there, but what does that have to do with me?

She and her little minions laughed like it was hilarious.

So, she had an audience?

 It wasn't very comfortable.

I'm sure it wasn't, Dawn, but -

So you're saying I shouldn't have done it?

You have a bright future, dear. Don't let someone who won't matter three years from now derail your purpose.

I fulfilled my purpose. I knew she was two-faced, and everyone could see her reflection now.

And you have three days away from school to reflect on that.

I'll probably get kicked off the volleyball team.

You might, which means you must explain that to several recruiters.

I messed up, huh, Dad?

Nope. You made a decision, and there's no rewind button.

I can't put the toothpaste back in the tube.

I bet that girl feels the same way.

Wuddya mean?

She lacked some judgment for a moment, and she will recall the choices she'd make in the future.

Well, we both made a memory in time; That's for sure.

That's right, but these hours at the food bank will act as time served in my book.

Whew. I thought you were going to take my phone away.

Nah. I'm not going to do that.

Thanks, Daddy.

Your mother already did. How's that for Wonky?

Very wonky.

RESET

You good?

I dunno.

Wuzzup?

I'm in a state of Blah right now.

What gives, Beaver?

Not sure, Wally. Really? You're calling me Beaver?

Trying to lighten up the mood.

I normally take a day to plan my month. I haven't done it.

Because?

I just told you. I'm in a state of BLAH.

'Splain, my dear.

I've just been in GO mode at work.

OK, it happens.

When I get home, I want to dedicate my time to you and Rusty.

As long as Rusty eats, has toys, and licks his balls, he's good.

Ew.

Not in that order, but don't put too much pressure on yourself.

Easier said than done.

You have 52 weeks in a year. It's OK to be off one or two.

I dunno.

I'm certain the universe will give you grace. Now, hug me.

You're so good to me.

Likewise, promise me to permit yourself to go with the flow.

I promise.

You are a joy. Sit still and let the seeds of life grow within you.

One day at a time?

No need to rush. It will be here within its own time and space.

Woo-sah.

Woo-sah.

SUBVENTION

I've got great news!

Let's have it.

I'm going to be a dad!

Congra- wait. What the heck did you just say?

You heard me. I'm gonna be a father.

Have you been kicking with someone no one knew about?

Nope.

What's that gal you met at happy hour? Sarah, right?

Not Sarah.

You are mad calm about this.

What's to be anxious about?

You're going to be a father. That part.

I ain't gonna have anything to do with the kid or kids.

Now that's fucked up on all kinds of levels.

Relax, relax.

Uh, relax? You're about to be a freaking father, man!

I know.

And, you're only freelancing. Can you afford this baby?

Most definitely! And I'm not freelancing anymore.

I need some clarification right now.

Well, you said it yourself, I was only a freelancer.

And?

And I needed some dough. Bad.

So?

So I made a donation.

You what?

I read an article that there's a sperm shortage in the UK.

The UK?

Yes, and I contacted the British Cryobank.

I must be trippin' on something in the air.

You? You wouldn't believe what I've been through.

Like?

Seriously. I was interviewed by 24 families, all via video chat.

How'd that work out for ya?

I went through a rigorous screening process.

Explain rigorous by way of video chat, please.

They asked about allergies, tattoos, and if I had any diseases, WOW.

Even asked if I contracted COVID too and get this.

I'm all ears.

21 out of the 24 families asked if I was at least 5'11.

Who wants a short kid?

I passed the exam and spent three days in Manchester.

You were flown to London?

Yep. Jacked off practically every other hour on the hour.

TMI

Yeah, I felt violated, and I was the one doing the violating.

Alright, alright, fast forward to the dad part.

My swimmers passed, and five families put a bid on my jizz.

Oh my god.

It's all legit. Couples can't produce, so I'm a donor.

Just a donor?

There's a law over there that I can be contacted 25 years from now, but there's no financial responsibility on my part.

I'm speechless.

Crazy right?

So, how many air quote kids will you have?

Maybe four, but possibly five if the other mother conceives.

Unbelievable.

Just congratulate me.

Congratulations. I guess.

NEXT UP

There is no perfect time to say this.

Oh, Lord.

Why are you bringing the Lord into this?

Just spit it out and tell me.

Goodness.

Have you been unfaithful to me?

Oh, you took it there?

Yes, I did.

Why is it that when a man says he has to say something, his lady thinks the worst-case scenario?

Because normally, it IS the worst-case scenario.

It's nothing like that.

So what is it?

I've been offered a job out of the state.

Are you serious?

I told you it wasn't perfect timing.

So what are you going to do?

It's just an offer.

Well, it must be a good offer.

It is. It is a great offer. Almost too good to be true.

If it's that good, something's up.

That's what my gut tells me, too.

Trust your gut.

I didn't get put in the ringer of interviews like my last two jobs.

Well, no one should have ten interviews for any job.

I think it's their way of testing one's resilience.

I look at it like dating. If you don't know there's a connection after the second or third date, there's no connection.

I'm surprised you say that. How many times did we go out?

Child, please. I knew about you and your shenanigans.

Shenanigans? Who have you been listening to?

My instincts.

And your instincts said what?

You were too polished, too smooth. All the right words to say.

Does my degree in Linguistics and Master's in Communications have anything to do with my usage of the English language?

Hmmm. You just seemed above the line all the time. Almost untouchable, which made you more desirable.

Oh really?

Yeah, but it wasn't sexy to me at all.

Of course, with all my shenanigans. The nerve.

When you told me you've been to seven countries, I just assumed you were a wild guy.

Skip well-traveled, cultured, critically conscious, astute, and diplomatic, huh?

Dang, since you put it that way. So what's next with this offer?

I'll sleep on it. I asked for a couple of days to respond.

Well, let's cuddle on it and decide in the morning.

Now that's a great offer.

Miss Understood

House and Home, Patrick speaking, how may I help you?

Am I on speaker?

Janelle?

Am I on speaker?

No.

Take me off the speaker!

You're not on speaker, and why are you yelling?

Am I some dumb bitch to you?

What?

Say it!

Say what?

You think I'm a dumb bitch!

I - I- I would never call you that. What's going on with you?

Just say it!

First, I don't use that word, and secondly, I did not call you that.

Janelle is a dumb bitch! Say it!

Listen, Jay, I don't know what-

Don't call me Jay! You think I'm some dumb bitch, don'tcha?

Are you drunk? Have you been drinking or something?

Maybe I am, but say what you think: I am a dumb bitch.

Is this a joke or something?

Do I sound like I'm joking?

Where is all this coming from?

You slept with Wachovia!!

What? Your best friend?.

Wachovia said you spent the night with her. How could you?

Wait, wait. You've got it wrong. Wachovia's mixing messages.

Oh, so you did sleep with her?

No. Hell No!

I'm the dumb bitch!?

Jay, uh, Janelle. Listen for a second.

What I did to you in your shower, I've never done to any man.

Much appreciated.

Now I feel like a dumb bitch!

If you can be quiet for 60 seconds, PLEASE!

You got 60 seconds. 59...58...

Wachovia stopped by the office, all freaked out. The security guard almost refused to let her up, but she said someone was following her. I told her we could call the police and meet them at her place. She asked me to follow her to her apartment. We went up and waited. It was already 2 in the morning, and I asked Wychovia for Tylenol. The girl gave me a PM pill, Janelle. I passed out on her couch. I didn't even hear the police arrive. Wachovia's dude came home, shook the shit out of me, and sent me on my way. I was still drowsy, so I slept in my car.

I'm gonna call and ask Percell about this!

I did not sleep *with* Wachovia. I slept *at* Wychovia's place. On Wychovia's couch until Percey told me to bounce.

Uh-huh. So why did that bitch lie to me?

I think the information was delivered incorrectly. That's all.

I'mma check that bitch.

Do what you have to do, Janelle.

You can call me Jay again.

YOU GOTS TO CHILL

Oh my goodness! Did you see that?

Yep. The dude fell right on his face.

Jesus. His friends aren't even helping him.

They're destroyed too.

How do you get that messed up?

I don't wanna sound like Cliff Clavin, but there's a science to it.

Oh yeah?

Alcohol stimulates the production of dopamine in your brain.

The what?

It activates the need to want more of what feels good.

Oh really?

Consequently, guys like broken face over there suffer.

Poor thing.

He doesn't know how to cut off that portion of his brain.

I thought it was 'beer before liquor and you'll never be sicker.'

The two ingredients are made from various chemicals

So what's that mean?

This means it results in crazy hangovers.

Aren't you a smarty at the party?

Meh. That question danced around in my head a few times.

Is that when you asked Cliff?

What?

Did Cliff tell you about the chemicals and the dopamine?

You're joking, right?

No, you said Cliff what's his face told you, right?

Clavin.

Yeah, Cliff Clavin.

Cliff Clavin from the TV show *Cheers*.

Never heard of it.

You've never seen Cheers?

Nope.

How bout we go to my spot and pull it up on Netflix?

And Chill?

And Chill.

That should create a dopamine reaction.

Undoubtedly.

SWIPE

How'd you like the party?

I had a good time. You've got cool friends.

Told you it would be fun.

Stephanie's a hottie. I'm surprised you two never hooked up.

Steph? Practically a sister to me.

Really?

I get it; she's smart, gorgeous, and doing big things.

She's doing well for herself.

I may have shot my shot once, but that was centuries ago.

Uh-huh.

Seriously. Plus, Steph's an engineer.

What's that mean?

She's a living, breathing computer.

I think I know what you're talking about.

Oh yeah?

Well, you guys were all glued to the TV watching the game.

Damn good game.

She went into why guys watch so many sports on television.

Uh oh.

It wasn't too crazy.

She's crazy.

Some science around our eyes being drawn to color, brightness, and motion.

That's not crazy.

She's definitely brilliant, interesting, and a hottie.

What's interesting, her guy Austin told us they met on an app. Ironic for an engineer to find the love of their life on an app, huh?

Austin said it freaked him out. She studied his profile.

You can find some cray-crays on apps. That's what I heard.

Steph created a program for three men she liked

Not surprised.

She used their intel to break down their conversations

WOW.

She tracked who would or wouldn't phone her back.

Stop playing.

Not playing. She analyzed their compatibility, and boom.

Boom?

Stephanie picked Austin.

WOW.

DOPPELGANGER
(by way of text message)

Yo, Rich, wuddup?

Wuddup?

Ain't nothing. u?

Same.

R U watching the game?

U know it

Surprised it's this close

Me too.

The defense is looking good.

MosDef

They gotta maintain though

Agreed.

I'm glad they traded Troutman

Bum!!!

Hothead too.

Should have traded him last yr

Messed up our playoff run.

Don't remind me.

U know Marty's @ the game.

Who?

Marty Blackwood.

I don't know Marty.

GTFOH

Y would I lie?

Dude, Marty B from Patty's party.

Patty?

Are you drunk?

Sober as a saint.

Really? U don't know Patty?

Promise. Don't know any1 named Patty or Marty.

Oh shit.

?

I texted the wrong Rich.

U should fix that.

My bad and U right. Adding last names.

No worries.

@ least U R watching the game.

Tru statement.

Good game too.

Xactly.

The defense is on point.

 U should text the other Rich.

LOL. Trudat

Peace

1luv.

Njoy the game.

Surprised it's this close

Me too.

RULES

Keith, can I get a ride home?

Sure

I appreciate it.

Car trippin again?

Don't get me started.

What's up with it now?

Get one thing fixed, something else breaks.

Damn.

I swear those mechanics are taking advantage of me.

If they fix it the first time, you don't have a reason to return.

That's a wack policy.

It's a terrible trick.

Damn shame is what it is.

You gotta check 'em from the door.

Facts.

Seriously. Ask for the manager or something.

They don't want that smoke.

Give 'em all the smoke.

Mmm, speaking of which, do you have a lighter?

Lighter for what?

My cigarette, silly.

Oh, nah, Tee, you can't smoke in my whip.

What. You actually mind if I smoke?

I don't mind that you smoke. I mind that you smoke in my whip.

Since when?

Ever.

I've smoked in your car before.

Negative.

I swear I have.

I beg to differ.

What about that time you drove me home from Applebee's?

We go to Applebee's a lot.

I know I smoked because they didn't let me smoke at the bar.

First, you can't smoke in any restaurant anymore.

I don't think I knew that.

And, I drove YOUR car. You were intoxicated beyond measure.

So you drove me home?

In your car.

And I smoked in my car.

It was your car.

I don't remember that.

As I said, you were drunkie-drunk.

Forget the cigarettes, I gotta stop drinking.

DESTINY'S CHILD

Tell me the story again.

How many times do I have to tell you this story?

It's so romantic.

Which part?

All of it.

Most of it isn't romantic.

What do you call it?

Spooky?

How bout romantically spooky?

Whatever.

Where were we?

When?

The first time?

First time? Paris.

Even that was romantic.

Geographically ironic.

Keep Going.

I missed the shuttle into the city, so I caught a ride.

And?

We went to a pub, and the locals didn't like military guys.

Not true.

We broke out before it got spicy.

They knew you'd take their women.

We just wanted to drink and listen to music.

I was at a party.

Indeed, you were.

I was there with my mom and my sisters.

Do you prefer to tell me the story?

No. Keep going.

I saw you. You saw me and I asked you to dance.

My mom wanted to dance.

So I asked your mom.

My mom still talks about that.

She enjoyed herself. We owned that floor.

Any man who takes care of my mother can take care of me.

You say that now. You weren't feeling me.

My sister was talking shit.

There is a term for that. She was hating.

An American soldier broke my mother's heart.

Glad she got over that.

Not really. Remember, I'm the only one who stayed in the States with Daddy. Esme and Amelle came back to France.

Correct.

So even that was fate.

I think the scary part of this is losing contact with you.

Aw, you missed me?

I'm stationed at Andrews, and I see you cheering at Howard.

Seeing you changed everything.

Yeah. We had to make some decisions.

No, YOU wanted to stay with that nappy-headed girl Katy.

I was supposed to just cut her off?

Yes.

Not fair, especially since you never returned my calls.

I thought we were a fling.

And I thought you were just getting your rocks off with an American soldier.

I kinda was. You were too good-looking to shoo away.

You never told me you lived in the States.

I was down to stay in contact, remember?

Nope.

Aww, come on, finish.

After seeing you, I couldn't stop thinking about you.

Me either. Seriously. I told all my friends about you.

It got so bad, Katy assumed I was cheating; she broke up with me.

Good riddance.

I don't understand how you dislike a person you never knew.

She delayed the process.

You have to trust the process.

Third time?

As they say, the third time's a charm.

Yasssss.

I'm stationed at McGuire in Jersey after my promotion to Captain. Rob is promoted to Captain and we drive up to New York to celebrate and who is at NYU for their master's?

Me.

Yes, you.

Rob insisted on getting a slice around Cooper Square.

Thank God for Rob and his addiction to New York pizza.

We're walking across the street, and I see someone who favors you, and Rob calls your name.

It scared me.

Imagine how I felt when you turned around.

You were beaming.

And I haven't stopped.

I love our story.

Happy Anniversary.

Happy Anniversary.

COMPROMISED

Ahh, that is the spot.
Does it feel good?
Absolutely.
I knew you'd like it.
This is incredible
Nice
I've never felt like this.
That's good to know.
Is that a bag?
Sort of. I call it a bubble.
Oh my goodness, this feels good.
That means I'm doing my job.
One helluva job.
Thank you.
Wha-what is that?
Hot wax.
Pulling out all the tricks, huh?
I got creative.
Spontaneity keeps things fresh.
I agree with you there.
Ahhh. This is wonderful
You're funny.
I'm just keeping it real.

You are into this, huh?

No doubt. Aren't you?

Of course. I'd do this even if I wasn't getting paid.

As the saying goes, you'll never work a day.

It works sometimes.

Raggedy people?

More like demanding.

Well, I'm enjoying this more than I thought.

Your wife paid for all of this.

What?

She said you never had a massage so she paid for the deluxe.

This is deluxe? I'd hate to know what premium is.

If you received the premium, you'd become a recurring client.

That good?

And then some.

Something that my wife knows about?

That is your decision.

WOW.

HOOK ME UP

Ayo, we here.

We? Who's we?

Me, Don, Rock, PJ

I can't get all y'all in, Black.

What. You said you got me.

I said I might have a ticket for you. YOU.

For real?

Plus, you brought three heads with you? C'mon, man.

We confirmed this over your DM

Yeah, I said I'll hitchu if I get a ticket.

I'm here.

How you bring a crew with you?

I roll with my crew all the time.

I can prolly get you in but not er'body else, yo.

Man, this is grimy, Nat.

What do you want me to do? This ain't my spot.

Get us in.

I'm just giggin here, Black.

I shot you a text.

I got no text, yo.

Check your phone.

I'm tellin' you, kid, I didn't get your text.

Look at your phone.

I'm looking. I don't see anything.

I sent it from a 2048 number. See it?

Nah.

I sent you a DM.

Fam, I ain't checkin' my DMs like that, especially if I'm working.

But I sent you a message.

Son, this says we coming through. Not me, we.

See? I sent you a message.

You and I never talked about tickets for WE.

This is crazy. What are we supposed to do now?

Go buy a ticket.

Man, you are lucky I got papers.

Papers? Are you trying to get gully over a ticket to a show?

Facts.

Are you threatening me?

Nah, I'm trying to do right, plus you, my dude.

Bet.

At least I thought you were.

I can't bump for four people, bro!

You played me, Nat.

Whatever. You played yourself.

PROPAGANDA

One week from Turkey Day. Are we hanging at your girl's? Don't call it that.

Call it what?

Turkey Day. They're not being celebrated, they're being eaten.

I knew I couldn't say Thanksgiving so I thought I'd switch it up.

Every year we get together to acknowledge a jacked-up history.

What do you do when everyone's hanging together 'giving thanks?'

I stopped trying to explain after my Columbus conversation.

I remember that. I think the Bears and Lions game paused.

Columbus was an idiot and Natives owned slaves.

You said the Natives were idiots for being called Indians.

We've been brainwashed for a long time.

Right, so why say something?

Tasha's people were pissing me off.

So you took it upon yourself to break the rank and file, not to mention prayer, to speak on it?

Perfect timing.

So are we going or not?

Everything about our lives has been a lie and all you're worried about is mac and cheese?

What the hell do you want me to do? It's one day. We can't fix all the shit by next week.

I'll just say I'm sick.

Great….then I'm stuck bringing you back food you won't eat.

More for you.

More for me.

CONTROVERTIBLE

When are you coming back?

Why?

I'd like to know.

Why? You didn't seem to care when I was there. Why now?

I can't get you off my mind.

You had me 24/7

I didn't know what I had.

Did your well run dry?

I wasn't seeing anyone else.

Technically, you were.

Really? Who?

Your sister. Your Mom. Your Job.

It is my job. What do you want me to do, Quit?

No.

Then what?

Adjust.

How about you adapt?

Interesting flip but I've been doing that.

Do some more.

I just love how you flip it to be about me.

You left. You chose to leave. So therein lies the flip

Shame.

What?

Nothing.

No, tell me.

Let's see how I can frame this.

While you're thinking, I just can't get us off my mind.

Oh really? Why now?

 Maybe this time has shown me something.

That is?

We're beautiful together.

That's what you think?

Yes and I don't want to think that you are out there wanting something more or someone new.

I've never wanted anyone other than you.

Your search history says something different.

As the saying goes, you'll find what you're looking for.

I wasn't looking for anything.

But you felt compelled to search my files?

I looked for clues. You left or vanished without any notice

I'm surprised you noticed.

That's not fair.

All that I feel for you, I just want us to be real with each other.

Just. Come Home. Please.

That's real.

TWICE THE FIRST TIME

Crazy what happened to Keysha.

Yeah, I know, shame.

She hasn't even been living here that long and bam.

At least no one was hurt.

Someone did get hurt. Tried shot.

What?

That's what she told us.

What happened?

There was a big argument outside her window. Just as she's peeking to see what's happening, bullets fly through her window. A couple lodged in her wall.

Jesus.

Right. She could have been hit by a stray and killed.

Makes ya wonder if she'll pack up and move back to Compton.

You mean Boston.

No Compton. Keysha's from Compton.

I'm not sure about that.

Keysha Cruz is from Compton

I'm talking about Keysha Perez. She is from Boston.

So this happened to Keysah Perez from Boston?

Yeah. Did something happen to Keysha Cruz from Compton?

Yes, but when did all this happen to Kesha from Boston?

Last night.

Incredible.

Did something happen to Keysha from Compton last night?

Yep. She was riding her bike and someone attacked her. Tried to take her bike.

Damn.

She maced the guy and cut 'em with a blade.

Good for her.

Not exactly. The thief pressed charges.

Get the heck outta here. Is that possible?

Possible as the cops showing up to arrest her.

Here at work? When did this happen?

Same as Keysha from Boston. Last night.

Lord, help us. How'd they know to come here?

Get this. Keysha from Compton filed a police report from the incident and it matched the mugger's story but he told them Keysha from Compton attacked him and stole HIS bike.

I know she didn't go out like that. That is just insane.

What's even more insane is that when they went to follow-up with the guy who filed the report, he got shot.

What?

Yeah, he was trying to steal someone's bike.

That must have been in Keysha from Boston's complex.

Wild night for them.

Even worse for that guy.

Karma.

NEW 2 THIS

Woo, the music was on point. I couldn't stop dancing.

I saw you getting your groove on.

You left me out there.

Trust me, you had plenty of company and dance partners.

But I wanted you out there.

Whatchu talkin' bout, I was out there housin' with ya for a lil bit

Then you dipped.

Someone had to watch your purse.

Thank you, Carter. That was quite noble. But you didn't dance.

Of course, I danced. I knew you were going to enjoy this space.

One of your lady friends checking on you?

Don't be like that, Morgan.

So, someone is here. You got a boo thang out there?

It's not like that.

Are you interested in someone or are they interested in you?

Can men say it's complicated?

Of course, especially if they're trying to avoid the question.

Touche'

Why so withdrawn about it?

Can I keep it real with you?

Yes by all means. Don't start being different with me now.

I'm feelin' someone but I'm not sure she's feeling me like that.

Have you spoken to her about it?

Not exactly.

You won't know how she feels until you share your feelings, C.

True.

Tell you what. Let's walk over there and you introduce us.

You want me to do what?

Then you can offer to get us drinks and let me feel her out.

That's the plan?

I know your type.

Oh, you do?

We've been friends long enough for me to know what you like.

This is going to be more difficult than I thought.

Dang, Carter. You're feeling this sista, huh?

For a minute.

So let's go over there.

Tell you what. You hang back

I can do that.

I'll bring us some drinks. I'mma take a leak first.

Make sure you wash your hands.

You got jokes.

What is this?

It's a long beach iced tea. I know you like fruity drinks.

Aw, you remembered; this is my favorite. Thank you.

My pleasure.

Wait. Where's the drink for your secret crush?

She's standing next to me, drinking a long beach iced tea.

What? Carter!

Morgan.

Carter.

Morgan.

I don't know what to say. We're like brother and sister.

I don't see it that way.

Why would you want to mess this up by getting us tangled?

If I'm gonna mess up, I'd prefer to mess up with you.

What if this gets messy?

At least I know we'll fix it fast.

You're just full of surprises.

So you wanna give it a go?

Only if you dance with me.

Done. Bring your purse.

DESPONDENT

Hey, how was the conference?

What is that smell?

Burnt popcorn.

Oh my goodness.

I don't think the people in the next suite ever got it right.

I don't know what's worse. Burnt popcorn or burnt bacon.

I'd eat burnt bacon before burnt popcorn

All the same to me. Did you call downstairs?

Didn't have to. The alarm went off and someone from management was up here. Professionally provided us with an update and told us not to worry about evacuating.

Superb.

So?

So?

The conference?

Oh. I'm over it.

Dang. Really? What happened?

Major disappointment.

You were looking forward to attending.

Yeah, I was.

Did you meet R.T?

Regrettably. It's true what they say about meeting your heroes.

That bad?

I can't put my finger on it.

What got you in a funk about meeting him?

His success as a writer allowed his books to adapt to some pretty dope movies and a tv series, but we didn't have to hear about it every five minutes. It seemed he highlighted his achievements more than anything and it got tired fast.

Was this during the panel discussion or the meet and greet?

Primarily the panel.

He is a celebrity. Hollywood has done a number on him.

The brotha used to be one of the real ones, ya know?

He was on the grind like us all and it paid off for him.

The money stole his grit.

How was he during the meet and greet?

Believe it or not, I gave my credentials to someone else.

I don't. You paid an extra 200 dollars for a meet and greet.

I went. Saw Dr. Stone there. She said Hello and was disappointed that you didn't accompany me.

She just wanted to see what I was wearing.

She's quite the dresser but you dress better.

Thank you, Dear, but you should have stayed.

I chopped it up with her most of the time and then I bounced. I gave my lanyard to a young writer who was waiting outside for an autograph.

Aww. You made a memory for him.

Right. The guy practically leaped in my arms.

That was super nice of you.

I just hope his admiration doesn't leave an impression like this burnt popcorn smell.

LOOSE ENDS

Hello!

Finally! You are one hard brother to track down.

I've gotten all your messages.

So no return call? This is the love I get after all these years?

You can thank Kianna.

Kianna?

She convinced me to take your call. What's so urgent?

We have a new road manager and before you say anything
- -

Nope. I'm done.

Come on, Manny! We need you. I need you.

Sorry.

 This is big, bro! We're going to open for Usher!

Usher? He's not even our generation.

I know, I know but Arnie - that's the new guy - says it will showcase our music to a different audience. By the sixth or seventh show, we'll - -

Sixth or seventh? Do you have dates?

Yeah, man! That's what I've been hitting you up for, doc! We got shows, we got dates and, you'll love this, we got advances.

So this is what this is about?

Well, it's a start. We can work out the details from the past issues regarding Tony and - -

Don't even spew his name; that punk motherfuh….look. I gotta process this. Lemme talk to Kianna. We're planning a trip to Portland to see her folks and things are going well for us now that this music bullshit is behind me.

I might have overstepped but I told Kianna.

You ain't shit, Kurt.

What?

Always thinking about you.

That's not true, brother.

You never consider anyone else's thoughts, plans, or feelings.

This ain't about me this time, brotha, and I apologize about the past; but it's about getting everyone paid and for real this time. Usher's camp loves the idea.

Has anyone seen or heard from that thief, Tony?

Let's put it like this. If Arman can't find him, he's off the grid. Maybe dead, even.

He better be. Usher, huh?

Yeah, man. We got like 24 shows. It's fantastic!

I'll do it on one condition.

You name it, brother.

I need what Tony stole from us. From me!

I mean, I can get you your advance money from the tour but….

I ain't talking about the bread we are about to make, Kurt!

Brother, I dunno how I'm going to recoup that kind of dough before we start this gig but I promise you I'll make it happen if you get down with us.

He set me back bad, Bro! I almost lost Kianna over that slimeball, Tony. You don't know how long it took me to get her back. I signed and sold my favorite ax.

I remember.

Apparently not.

Well, I saw it online. You weren't taking anyone's calls.

I didn't know who was in cahoots with that bastard!

How much to make it right, Manny?

Twenty.

Wooh! Look, I'll get it but it's gonna be a couple of days to move some funds around.

You do that and I'm in, bro.

Right on! I can't wait to tell the crew.

Usher, huh?!

Usher, Baby!

Let's do it.

VARIETY

Hey, can we talk?

Uh-oh.

No, it's nothing like that. I just wanted to talk about a little thing.

A little thing.

Yeah, it's not a big deal but it's something I've noticed.

Is something the matter?

No, not really.

Just tell me.

OK, we're both neat freaks; and that's fine.

Oh, I got it now.

Do you because I don't want to make this a thing.

Whatever's bothering you is making it a thing so tell me.

The silverware drawer should be forks, knife, then spoon.

I didn't know it mattered.

Yes, I'm grabbing forks for my oatmeal.

Lemme see. Oh. I'm putting them as spoon, knife, and fork.

Exactly.

OK.

So you get my drift?

You're grabbing forks for oatmeal and not spoons.

I am accustomed to the spoons being right here.

Do those lovely Tom Fords allow you to see spoons?

Oh, we're going there?

I'm just saying; well, you're saying you're not making it a thing.

I'm not.

But you are.

I really don't think I am.

Open the drawer, look down, and get a spoon.

It's not that simple.

I think it is.

And you don't have to flare your eyebrows when you say that.

Now it's my eyebrows and not the forks and spoons?

It's the way you're patronizing me about the silverware order.

The order that's not a thing but really a thing?

Forget it.

No, no, lemme go rearrange the drawer.

Don't worry about it

Oh no. I got it. This is definitely a thing.

Don't be like that.

God forbid we don't want oatmeal on the floor.

Why would oatmeal be on the floor?

Fork?

Now you are making it a thing.

Ha! Not me.

FOXY & FILTHY

You are super sexy like a Pam Grier kind of vibe.

You're sweet.

I mean it. I still watch those throwback flicks.

Well, I've been waiting for this for as long as I can remember.

Get out of here.

You're fine and you don't even know it which is a turn-on.

I appreciate that.

Women my age, you know, like young men.

I didn't know. I thought I was attractive but. . . thanks, I guess?

Why are you stopping? Don't stop. Keep going.

I can talk and do this at the same time.

I can't. This is . . . this is some good…oh my god.

Do you like it?

Yes. Please stop talking.

They talk like this in some of those movies.

What movies? Just stop talking and give . . . give it

Right there?

Give it to….ooooh, yes, right there.

Right there?

Right there.

Harder?

Harder, harder.

Faster?

No. Scoot to the edge of the bed and put my legs on your shoulders

OK, Miss flexible. We're going there.

Stop talking….I'm almost there.

Good…I'm ready to bust.

Not yet….oooh, yes…so, so, good.

Its good. Real good.

Just…..just… like that….ohhh my gaaaawwwd. I'm….I'm….I'm

Oh my god!

Oh my god!

Ohhhhh? What in the . . .

Ooooooh

Noooo! Nooo!

What? What's the matter, baby? Why did you stop?

Oh my god; I'm going to be sick.

What happened, baby?

You don't see it? You don't smell it? I'm gonna throw up.

Oh my…oops… I'm so sorry.

Oops? This is foul. It….its all over me.

Lemme help you.

No. I gotta shower. I'm gonna be sick.

Yes, get in the shower and I'll clean this up.

This puts a new spin on letting loose. I'm gonna be sick.

SLIDE THROUGH

Hola, Mami. Como estas? You Up?

Hola, Papi Chulo. Mi amigo sexy en la ciudad.

There you go. You know I don't know what you said.

Esa es la parte divertida. Que Pasa, Papi?

You know, chillin, thinking about you. You up?

I'm talking, ain't I?

I'm saying though.

You're so cute when you're horny.

You think you know me. Slide through.

It's too cold out there, Papi.

I'll warm you up once you get here.

I don't like coming over there by myself at night, baby.

It ain't all that bad. I'll meet you at the door.

You know they call your area New Jack City, right?

I got you. I'm burning your favorite incense.

The last time you did that you almost burned the place down.

I moved the potpourri dish away from the ashes. Come through

I don't know, Papi. How bout you come over here?

Really? Your crazy-ass tia ain't gonna flex on me?

She and my Abuela went to the casino until tomorrow.

I'm throwing my Timbs on right now.

Bring some Sambuca.

Damn, Mami, you know that makes you wild, right?

You know you like it wild, especially with my toys.

Don't write a check you can't cash.

I'm going to season a steak for breakfast.

I'll try not to get a ticket speeding over there.

Don't do that, Papi. Cops got no love for brothers.

And neither does your tia.

Well, my tia ain't here so darse prisa, Papi!

DIFFERENT KIND OF PARTY

Paulie, you busy?

What's good, my guy?

Its poppin!

What's poppin?

Son! I got some thing-things coming through for a party.

Word? You got a party poppin?

No doubt. Drinks flowing, Jamaican food, fine breezies.

Cool. What time are you doing things?

Man, I'm getting started NOW.

I see that; your energy is mad high for 11 in the morning.

Yeah, man. You know how I do it.

OK. Well, lemme get this workout done and I gotchu.

I did a few rounds in the ring and realized the date

Right on. You got a big heart. I like that about you.

Manscaped because the shoobie-doobies like it tidy.

Alright, Bruh you buggin.

It's a celebration, Fam! You gotta be on point for spontaneity.

Cool. You may have to slow down a lil bit, bro.

I'm gully.

 You're gonna be sloppy when the guests slide through.

True, true but we're celebrating.

Gotcha. I'll slide through. Should I bring anything?

HoneyBunz likes those little fuzzy mice. You can bring that.

HoneyBunz? Like your cat, HoneyBunz?

Yeah. It's HoneyBunz's birthday! We getting it in for her.

Are you serious?

Dead-ass.

I can't rock witchu on this one, fam.

STAY READY

My brother, my brother. How long has it been?

Too long. Now that you are married with kids and shit.

Oh, don't put that on me. You're the famous TV guy now.

It's just a gig, bro. Just a gig.

Pfft. I tell people I know you and I get all kinds of reactions.

I'm sure. I have a fair share of fans and fanatics.

Uh, haters. People are wild on Twitter, IG and what's it called?

I still call it Facebook but Meta.

Right. Meta. Some people flat out want your head removed.

Let 'em come.

You're not afraid? I mean, we're out in broad daylight.

So?

So, anybody come run up on us and steal on you.

First of all, you forgot who you talking 'bout. It's me, ya boy!

True but when you hit celebrity status, folks are obsessive.

I'm just doing a job. They don't like it, turn the friggin channel.

They want to hear what you're going to say.

Which means, I'm doing a good, damn job, right? Right!

I just want you safe out here in these streets, bro.

Look over there. See my man hanging by the newsstand?

Big Dude? Yeah, what about him?

He's with me or he's with us.

Word?

I'm a commodity to the network. I gotta be protected.

Damn. Is anybody else undercover around us?

Yep. My man at the table behind us. He's got the heat.

I would have never known, bruh, but you *are* famous now.

Look, I can hold my own. All facts though. Fools are crazy.

As I said, those tweets are menacing.

And someone is always close in case something goes down.

Stay ready so you don't have to get ready.

That's my mantra.

NINE-TENTHS OF THE LAW

You still mad?

Yes.

Aw, Don't be mad, sugar-wooga.

Don't try to sweet-talk me?

So you are not talking to me?

No, not really.

You're mad because I used your soap.

Yes, and why are you using my stuff anyway?

Your stuff?

Yes. Please stop using my soap.

Your soap?

You know you have been using my soap.

How do you know?

I know how my soap smells and you smell like it.

Your soap is in MY bathroom.

No, it's OUR bathroom.

Our bathroom?

Yes, dammit, our bathroom?

Then it's our soap then.

No, it's not.

OK, cool. I'm going to Cold Stone and get ME some ice cream.

Really?

Are you talking to me now?

I mean you didn't say you were going to Cold Stone.

The great equalizer.

Smart-ass.

Better than a dumb-ass.

See? Comments like that keep me mad at you?

Using your soap keeps you mad at me.

Whatever. Birthday cake in a waffle cone?

I'll think about it. Lemme go wash up first.

You betta not!

NOT A FAN

Hey, girl.

Hey. Whatchu up to?

Would you believe I'm just unpacking from our trip?

I washed everything yesterday you're not by yourself.

That's refreshing.

I had a blast though. I think we all needed it.

Shoot. Who are you telling?

Everybody.

If I didn't do something soon, Derrick would've been missing.

Girl, you're crazy but I understand.

Did you hear from anybody else?

Chloe said James was practically pushing her out the door.

Hmmm, James probably had a trip of his own planned.

All the husbands and boyfriends prolly did.

James certainly did.

Don't be like that. He's atoned for his errors.

Whatever.

Be nice. Plus, it could not match our trip, regardless.

Riiiight.

And for the forty-tenth time, your body, girl.

Thanks.

You've been getting your workout on.

Thank my trainer, Oscar. I wanted to look good in our pictures.

Pffft. You always look good.

Speaking of which.

What's up?

Can you delete that last pic of us on the beach?

What? Girl, you look flawless in that picture.

I don't like it.

What don't you like about it?

My hair is in my face.

You look good in that picture, Faye. All the pictures!

Do you think so?

Yeah, I just think you're looking at it too much.

Hmmm. Can you just delete that one pic?

No.

Really?

I'm pretty sure, I showed you the picture after we took it.

But you didn't say you were going to post it.

I post everything.

That you do.

Wow.

Why are you in your feelings now?

The comments are all about you.

Say what?

Ah, you know you read the comments.

I'm not a fan of what people say in the comment section.

So why am I deleting the picture?

Because I don't like it.

It's my page.

Please?

It's got a lot of likes.

Really?

Everyone's vibing on your curls. Check the comments.

I'll take your word for it. I don't do comments.

So the picture stays.

I guess.

THE GAMBLE

How much did that put you back?

Less than I thought after my military discount.

Nice. I'm glad stores do that.

Me too. I asked and they said they'd honor it.

I think she's gonna love it.

I hope so.

Look at that thing. It's mad, nice. I don't know jack about rings.

I did some research on the cut, color, grading, and clarity.

I'm impressed, man.

You're supposed to spend like twice your salary, right?

Don't believe the hype.

It's all hype, right?

Right. Get what you can afford. It shouldn't matter.

Size matters, though.

Once again, get what you can afford.

It's a decent size, right?

It's basically an overpriced promise ring if you ask me.

What did Raina say when you proposed?

Uh, Yes?

I know she said yes, but was she happy with the ring?

If I could put Vikings season tickets around her finger instead of a ring, she married me on the spot.

I forgot your lady is sports junkie. You married an alien.

A sexy alien if I might add.

Q&A

How long have you and Benjamin been together now?

Three years.

That's beautiful and he is great with Lil Tre.

That's what made me fall for him. He treats Tre like he's his.

I saw y'all at church. The little family. So sweet.

But….If you could have seen all the eyes on us.

Whatcha mean?

Anthony's family attends the first service as well.

Oh. Well, no one told Anthony to be the kingpin of the capital.

Girl, please.

What? He put you and Tre's life at risk.

The scariest chapter of my life.

Yours? I saw all those cop cars.

I had no clue Anthony was involved like that.

Are you sure about that?

What are you saying?

Either you've been blind or had your eyes closed.

I beg your pardon?

What kind of work did you think he did?

He owned two salons for men and women.

Do you believe two barbershops paid for your lavish lifestyle?

All them weaves and braids getting done?

That's a lot of horsehair, girl.

I admit I speculated something was up but...

But?

I didn't want to assume.

Assume what? He ain't washing money?

Lots of ballers are in and out of those shops all the time.

How about when the battering ram smashed your front door?

Where are you going with all this?

I just don't want you to lose Benjamin. He's a good man.

I know.

And I don't expect Anthony to get out any time soon.

I know that also.

I'm just saying, girl.

What made you ask me all of this anyway?

I have to pass your block to get to the grocery store.

And?

And I was going to stop by and say Hello.

I was home, you should have.

I know. I saw your Jeep.

You should've sent me a text or called me.

You ever noticed a Crown Victoria parked under a big tree?

Across the street from me? All the time.

Ever wonder why it's there?

Its just a car. Where are you going with all this?

I think the feds or some agency is watching your house.

Girl, you trippin.

I didn't want to say anything. Why are they still on you like this?

Stacy. You're paranoid.

Me? I don't have an unmarked car parked near my house.

What's this have to do with me and Benjamin?

I'd hate for him to get caught up in your shit.

My shit?

Yeah if you're somehow still involved in Anthony's business.

You're acting real sus' right now, Stacy.

Huh?

Are you wearing a wire?

Girl, you've been watching too much HBO or Starz.

What's with the questions?

I care about you, Lil Tre, and your relationship with Benjamin.

Look. I'mma keep it one hundred with you but it stays here,

Of course.

Anthony asked me to come to visit him with lil Tre. Understandable.

I hadn't visited Anthony since he's been locked up. I refused.

I don't blame you, after all that drama.

He heard I was seeing Benjamin. Said he was happy for me.

What else could he say? He locked up.

I know he was crushed. I could see it in his eyes.

Deserves it.

His momma and his sister must've prepared him.

All the eyes at church. I get it now.

Right. He wanted to tell me face-to-face he was OK with it.

What choice does the ninja have?

Not a lot.

He's in there for how long, 18 years?

Something like that. Since then, the Crown Vic has been there.

Do they think Anthony put you on or something?

Maybe. Maybe not. No one's knocked on my door.

That's good.

Plus, I've been maintaining my regular routines.

Hmm.

I cannot put Tre in any danger, Tracy. Benjamin either.

 I hope he pops the question. You need a fresh start.

Anthony needs to see his son.

As I said, that ninja is in jail. What is he gonna do if you move?

I don't want to find out.

So you did know?

I knew Tracy. I knew.

Dang.

Where's the reset button when you need it in real life?

THROWBACK

Yo! Are those Shelltoe Adidas?

I had to do it.

Man, those are classic.

I got the white ones and the classic sweatsuit too.

Oh, you're going all the way back.

Fa'sho. I miss those days. Not a care in the world.

Oh, you cared about Sissy back in those days, remember her?

How do I not remember? Her brother Don used to terrify me.

Sissy had that big-girl body even at 15 and her brother knew it.

Bruh, she was just pretty to me.

She was pretty to everybody.

I loved her smile and those dimples. I don't recall her frame.

You don't remember Sissy's booty?

Of course, I do.

Right, we all do.

I'm just saying I wasn't thinking about her like that back then.

Well, Donnie didn't know what you were thinking.

I swear that dude chased me for a mile before he stopped

He didn't catch you though.

I wasn't wearing shell toes that day either.

Oh yeah, it would've been a wrap for you.

THE STRUGGLE

Tobias Walker!

Alexandria Parker!

Long time.

Yep. It has been,

When's the last time you were back here?

Jeez. It had to be back in 09.

Right. For Monty's funeral?

Had to come back for that.

But then you disappeared.

Not much to return to with Monty gone.

So sad. I'm sorry.

Long time, but being back brings back memories.

It's finally good to see you, Mr. Walker

You as well, Miss Parker

It's Parker-Stevens now.

Ooh, yes; that's right. All fancy with the hyphenation.

Whatever.

How much convincing did it take for Mr. Stevens' to agree?

To the dash?

Yeah, most brothers don't dig the dash.

He was supportive of the name that made me famous.

Famous?

Yes, famous.

How bout Popular?

Popular? Popular is a high school fad.

How bout well-known?

I'm more than well-known, Tobias.

If you say so.

I've spoken at 39 colleges and universities, three prestigious tech firms, and fortune 100 companies and have been on Good Morning America twice.

Hmm. Was that before or after you stole my idea?

Your idea?

I didn't stutter.

OK. It was your idea but I engineered it into something big.

Big, huh?

Bigger than you would have done.

You don't know that.

Prove it.

A few of my notecards mysteriously disappeared and - -

This is what we're going to do?

What?

The first time we see each other and you're still on this?

Alex.

Tobias.

Alex.

Tobias.

Forget it, Alexandria.

No… let's not forget it.

Seriously.   Congratulations on all your success with MY idea.

Your idea?

I knew I shouldn't have attended this bullshit.

No, no. We're going to settle this right now.

We're grabbing people, now?

I apologize. Pardon me. It's just - -

What are we going to do, Alex? Turn back the clock? Go back in time to my apartment? Unsmoked the weed, put all our clothes back on, and not discuss the project that I was submitting to Dr. Jefferies?

We were working on it together, Toby.

Talking about it isn't working together.

It didn't happen that way.

It sure as shit and coincidently seemed that way, Alex

How do you view it?

You get a 20-grand fellowship, and poof, you're gone.

No, no.

Yes. You bounced before your toothbrush could dry.

I swear it didn't happen like that.

Dr. Jefferies sang your praises like you walked on water!

I had to take the opportunity that was presented to me, Tobias.

And people say men are dogs.

What?

You ain't shit and be glad I ain't the type of brother to drag you.

Drag me?

Or better yet introduce myself to your husband.

Well, that's really mature.

I know the real you.

You used to know me.

Facts. Keep being Mrs. Parker hyphenated fucking Stevens!

Tobias!

BETTA THAN THE ALTERNATIVE

Do you know why you're here?

Nope

No clue?

I know I want to play ball.

Do you think this will serve as your opportunity to do that?

Everyone told me I'd be in jail or dead so this place will do.

Fine but do you know why you're visiting me?

Man, I don't know. I guess you're the guy who will say it's cool.

Your academics are quite impressive while housed at Higley.

Housed, huh? Is that a new word for locked up?

Your actions required you to be detained.

Housed, detained; lots of identifiers for a dressed-up trash pit.

That's amusing.

But you ain't laughing.

Higley allowed you to showcase your athletic abilities.

No one could stop me.

Combined with the scholastic capability, you can recapitulate both at James Baldwin Prep.

I'm assuming that word you used means I can play ball here?

Assured there are no more additional infractions.

Infractions. like what.

One that potentially results in major consequences.

I'd go back to Higley?

Unfortunately, you are out of strikes so to speak.

Really?

Higley is no longer an option.

That's a'ight. I got people in Sanford. They'll look out for me.

Let's not become distracted by what could happen

True statement. One hundred percent.

Fantastic. Finally an amicable foundation.

Where you from, man?

Why does that matter where I'm from?

I'm sitting across from a black man, but you are making stuff sound more difficult than it should with your phrases and shit.

Interesting interpretation though your analysis of me is off-put.

See? That shit.

You know, we can expedite this conversation.

OK. Do it. Whatcha wanna know?

How did you end up in Higley?

Got caught.

Before being apprehended and sentenced.

Did what I had to do. You wouldn't understand, 3-piece suit.

Continue.

No Pops. Mom's high and overwhelmed with 5 starving kids.

What led to the lifestyle? You're an incredible ballplayer.

You ain't listening, Man.

Continue.

We were living in the dark, no heat, no hot water, no food, and high school ball wasn't keeping the lights on!

It is notably commendable you assumed head of the house with all that responsibility. Why not find legitimate work?

I ain't flippin burgers or stacking boxes when I know what's what on the block.

Understood.

Do you?

What do you think?

I think you're over there sitting in that leather chair judging me.

I was born and raised in Bed-Stuy, Brooklyn, New York City.

I don't believe you.

Father was present but absent with parenting skills.

Yeah? At least you knew your pops.

I like to say, he didn't know how to accurately love, and conceivably he loved too much.

What did he do, touch you or something?

Nothing like that; far from it. I met my two half-sisters from the Bronx and my half-brother from Spanish Harlem at his funeral.

Dang. Player, player.

I was in my doctoral program when I met them.

Oh, so you didn't have time for your new half-blood because

you were getting ready to read minds and shit, huh?

I needed as much closure as my new siblings did. I was able to surmise my theory of why I did not see him much as a child.

How did he die?

Not certain.

Mine got shot in Brownsville.

Unfortunate.

Say less.

No one should experience the trauma you have endured.

You don't know the half, man.

I cannot imagine your stress at Higley.

Better than the alternative.

I'm here to help you get through this so let's get you enrolled.

You're human after all. Respect.

Bless up.

CALI ROLL'IN

So,there's no raw fish in this roll?

No, I promise.

So what's the fishy taste I'm tasting?

Its crab meat.

Like a crab cake?

Sorta, kinda.

I gotta give it to you, you've turned me on to some new stuff.

Its my pleasure.

For real, I wouldn't have been caught in a place before you.

Speaking of which…..

What's good?

Its been five months -my friends have noticed us together a lot.

Your friends, huh?

They don't see me as much because you and I are together.

What, they don't have dudes?

Some do.

Lemme guess; the ones who don't are asking?

They're all asking.

Asking what?

Are we - you and me - kicking it or . .

Or?

Or….are we a couple?

A couple? We've known each other like 80 days, shorty.

Its been five months.

Not in a row.

So are we kicking it?

I dunno; I guess.

Are you seeing other people?

Actually . . .

I knew it, I knew you were . . . .

Can I finish?

Not if you're going to say you got other women.

What?

And let's not forget your son's mom.

She good people. We're amicable and she got a man. He cool too.

So what were you going to say?

Its like…its like this sushi spot.

What's the sushi spot gotta do with other women?

I'll explain. Fix your face. You ain't gotta cry.

I'm not crying.

I've been losing interest spending time with other women since

Since we been kicking it?

Yeah. I prefer to say, spending time together.

So what do I tell my friends.

Tell them you're happy and to mind their business.

You're something else, you know that?

We good over here! Spending time together.

I'm rollin with you.

Say less.

FUDDY DUDDY

Wow! New Whip?

Yes, Indeed. Do you like it?

It's dope AF but, er, uh, does your fiance' like it?

So you heard?

Of course, I heard. Are you familiar with social media?

Yeah, yeah.

The hardware looks like you won the world series.

Go Big or Go Home.

True. Looks nice on you.

This could have been -

Don't.

What?

Don't go there. Just don't. This is a real chilled vibe so, no.

Right, right. My bad.

So what's up? Why the urgent message to meet anyway?

Urgent?

Was this your way of breaking the news?

You didn't answer my calls or texts.

Should I?

No. I'm sure you heard from somebody.

So?

So; this is a little awkward.

What's more awkward than our meeting? And why now?

Plenty. How have you been?

Quit stalling and spill it.

OK. I'll spill it

Thank you, Jesus.

Don't be like that.

Spill it.

You know Tamia? You've been crushing on Tamia for years.

She and her sisters were your BFFs and I fell back.

Mmmhmm. We did a mini getaway thing in San Diego.

Mini?

I'm doing one with all my bridesmaids in Cabo next February.

That should be dope. So this trip was just a typical be-out.

Exactly.

OK.

The liquor was flowing AND the parties were great.

It's a nice vibe there if you know where to go.

Plus, we're getting all the eyeballs.

You do realize that will happen hanging with triplets.

They're my besties.

They could've hailed from wherever Wonder Woman is from.

Themyscira.

What?

Themyscira is the island where Diana Prince was raised.

Duly noted and I'll contact my travel agent tonight.

Silly.

Back to the parties. Did something happen?

That's the thing.

Uh oh.

All signs, all roads, and all systems were a-go but.....

But?

I couldn't go through it even though I was tipsy.

Hey, you're about to get married. Makes sense to me.

Hmm.

Are you getting cold feet?

Far from it. I'm happy, I'm ready, he's great and.....sorry.

An apology is not necessary. Glad you're happy.

Yeah, but still.

Your super ring was the call sign. It probably attracted hoes.

I know that, silly. That's not what I'm saying.

Whatcha saying?

Tracy was getting her groove on.

Figured. What's different?.

The other girls disappeared. I was ready to get gully too.

OK, big girl!

But

Did you chicken out?

I just didn't want it to be with some random brotha.

I see.

Now you get it.

No. Random, strange, or a jump-off is what it's supposed
to be.

True. I kept thinking if I'm going to do this, it's gotta be with you.

Me? Nah.

Nah?

Nah. I ain't going there.

Well, this is some BS.

Who do you think you are?

What?

Just hit me up, huh?

Well.

Soil your oats like Coming to America?

We have history and I'd rather it be you.

This is bananas. I don't even know why I came here.

No. Please. Sit. I think deep down you're with it.

Fuck my feelings, huh? What about your husband?

He ain't my husband yet.

Pffft. Do you hear yourself?

I'm still the one that can do that thing you used to like.

Are you kidding me?

You still like that, right?

Your chapter in my book is over. Trust me, it will permanently be one of my favorites but I can't keep re-reading it hoping for a modified conclusion. I'm out. Good luck with your party, your nuptials, and your life. Lose my number for real this time.

REMEMBER THE AVE?

Hey, do you remember Nadine Bransford?

Yeaaaah, I remember Nadine. How is she doing?

According to her pictures, fine but I don't remember her.

You remember her, dude. We used to call her Dina.

We could have called her Latifah. I don't remember her.

You're kidding, right?

I promise you, fam. I don't remember her.

Why are you asking about her anyway?

She sent me a friend request.

That was cool of her.

Not cool if I don't remember her.

Did you see any pics of her and her family?

That's what I'm saying, Bro. I don't recognize her.

C'mon.

What should I do?

I'm telling you, you know her.

I take your word for it.

Cool. Hit her up.

What purpose do I have to accept her request?

Dude, it's Dina.

You're not convincing me.

If she saw you and recalled a story of us, you'd be shook.

I get that but what do we have in common now? Like real-time.

Just a connection of one of yo friends from back in the day. What does that say about the friendship if I don't remember?

It says a lot about you.

Bruh, we're like in our 40s now. When did we hang with Dina?

High School.

Exactly. High School.

Doesn't change the fact that she's good peoples.

I don't know her like that anymore.

Why so tense?

I'm not tense. Too many people are holding on to the past like it contains magic powers.

People just trying to stay connected, Bro.

Connected? To what?

The world is changing.

True but make new memories.

Gotta cherish the fun times.

We had fun but we forgot about the other times.

Whatcha saying?

Ahmad Watson.

What about him?

Seven guys from Emmerson stomped him and left him for dead.

That was a long time ago.

Was Dina around?

She didn't have anything to do with that.

Dina's brother led the Emmerson Crew.

Wow, Bro. So you do remember her?

I recognized her brother in one of her posts.

See?

Same babyface.

OK.

Can reconnecting with her bring Mack back?

Low blow, man.

Here's one, Dee Simmons' house that caught on fire

Huh?

I click Dina's request, the kerosine tank doesn't explode, right?

Alright man, damn! Don't accept her request but stop bringing up old depressing shit.

My point exactly. I connect with Dina and/or anyone from the Ave and it's a wrap. All the ghosts return.

THING THING

I appreciate the hospitality, man. This was a great escape. Anything for you, fam. This was long overdue.

Yes, sir, Your lady Tabby is fine, man. Where'd you two meet?

Tabby is not my lady, fam. She's just a friend.

A friend? The way y'all were boo'd up. Not co-signing that.

Well, a friend-friend.

Right, because a friend-friend stays over and cooks in the AM.

Facts.

So she's your girl?

Nah, man. She's not my girl-girl, but my people, you know?

That's a head-scratcher. You don't kick it with your people.

Well.

Plus, I thought Gloria was your people.

Gloria *IS* my folk but Tabby is my people.

I don't get it. I do but I don't. Maybe, I just don't, Yeah, I don't.

It ain't that hard. Gloria's like a sister. We cool.

Y'all cool-cool or just cool?

Nah. Me and Gloria and just cool.

And she's your folk?

Right. My folk-folk.

Oh, I get it now.

You sure?

Yep. Tabby's the body and Gloria's the brain.

I don't think I would have put it that way.

C'mon. You're smashing Tabby and it's casual, right?

Fa'Sho.

But Gloria is your intellectual friend who you don't want to lose.

OK. That's acceptable. I can see that with your glasses.

Do I have to explain it to you? They're your friends!

They're my people. My folk.

Forget it. I'm out, Bro.

FRESH OUT

Cornelius Ulysess Danielson!

Only my momma can call me that and you missing tits.

I have known you for 960 months, bro. I can call you whatever.

Sho' can if you want your face disfigured.

Right here outside the wall? Might as well make an about-face.

Ain't going back in there, my dude. Ever!

Well, give me some love, Cuddy!

That's more like it. Cuddy is back, baby!

And swole like Deebo! RIP to Tiny.

Yes. That movie has a body count longer than some inside.

How was it being inside with bonafide killers?

Sheeeeeit, man, half of 'em know me. The other half ain't flex.

That's good.

Having damn-near a band on my books from the git helped.

I heard that commissary life was real.

It can make you or break you into itty-bitty pieces.

Speaking of itty-bitty, you want me to drop you off at Carla's?

I'll see Carla tonight. I need to register with the P.O.

Right now?

Orders.

Alright, bro, just tell me where but we gon' get litty tonight.

Lemme think about that.

Think about it? Everyone's gon' be at your house tonight.

I got something to do.

Oh, they got Daytimer Planners in the joint now?

Hey, man, chill with all that.

The entire crew is waiting to see you.

I just need to clear my head before I see everybody.

Watcha' wanna do?

See this P.O. and drop me at the beach. I need to reconnect.

I don't get it.

You wouldn't. I don't expect you and anybody else to get it.

SOCIAL BUTTERFLY

We're heading to the cigar bar. Wanna meet there?

Nah, bro, I'm cool. I don't do cigars like that.

You don't smoke cigars?

Nope.

Hmm, I could have sworn I saw you smoking a stick.

I had one when Chuck's daughter was born but different flow.

So you do smoke?

Not really. Special occasions. I hardly finish them.

So you wouldn't know the difference between - -

The difference between a 2-dollar stick or a 20-dollar stick.

So what do you do on the golf course?

I don't golf.

Hold up. You don't golf?

I've been out there with Chuck because he doesn't judge me.

It ain't about judging you, bro. Its the camaraderie.

I can do that at the bar or at Chuck's spot.

Yeah, Chuck has a helluva deck. Which whiskey do you drink?

Not into liquor all that much. I like beer though.

I feel like I'm learning more about you than I knew before.

I'm still the same person. I just don't smoke cigars.

That's strange. Everybody smokes cigars now.

Which is probably why I don't. Feels like a fad to me.

So, you're the odd man out at the party with no stick.

I can still indulge in cordial conversation without a cigar, bro.

I don't know, man. Seems weird to me.

Personal choice. No different than not smoking cigarettes.

Right. Those things'll kill ya.

CONDOLENCES

Hey girl; did you hear?

Yeah. I'm a mess about it.

Me too. Did you call Brooklyn yet?

No. I'm weird about calling. It's like what can you say or do?

I thought it was just me. I started my text like eleventeen times. Exactly.

Well, we gotta do something. We're her girls.

I know, I know. How 'bout we facetime her together?

I like that.

Then she can let us know if she needs us to do anything.

Wonderful idea

Is it too soon?

Gosh; I was thinking that same thing.

We gotta do something. I know she's not thinking straight so…

So we should just go over there.

Right, right. Show her some love in person.

And Benji too.

Oh my goodness, Ben. I totally forgot. I know he's a mess.

Yeah, girl. I just don't know what to say to either of them.

I think just being there for them will matter.

OK. Lets pick up some food from Panera or somewhere.

Girl, Ben ain't eating Panera. You better get some fried chicken.

OK, chicken for Benji and soup and salad for Brooklyn.

Is that Vegan shop open yet?

Yes, I'll stop there.

That'll do it.

Come get me.

Me?

Who else?

I thought you were getting me?

Does this have to be a production? It's for Brooklyn.

OK….on my way.

VIVA

I'm going to go on record and say this is my first Day Party.

Really? They're pretty fun.

Right. Who knew?

The music is great. They can get wild.

What? With youngsters living their best life?

Hey, sometimes you'll see cougars hunting for cubs.

WOW. Like old boy over there. He's gotta be twice her age.

Oh shit.

What?

That's my ex.

Get outta here. Are you for real?

I don't think anyone else has a hideous lion tattoo like that.

Sharp-looking fella. What happened between you two?

Exhibit A right before your eyes. He likes them young.

We don't have to stay. There's another party somewhere else.

Oh no. We're going to enjoy this music and vibe out.

You sure?

Absolutely. In fact, he'll probably leave if he sees us.

Wanna dance and make him jealous?

We can dance but not put on a front or something.

I feel a lil weird knowing your ex is over there.

Don't. It's been a while; a couple of years so it's cool.

Weird and wild coincidence. Of all places, right?

The conference happens to be in Vegas this year, not L.A.

True statement. The big dogs wanna get wild.

Nothing's as it seems. They get wild everywhere.

I think he recognized you. He's looking over here.

He won't come over here. Not while you're here.

Oh, he's one of those guys, huh?

What kind is that?

Secure until he's faced with his own insecurities.

Interesting.

He's the happiest thinking you're home crying about him.

Screw it; let's dance!

THE BEHOLDER

Jules, it's been 3 months and you haven't called me back.

You told me to take my time.

Yeah, but I didn't think it was going to be a fricking quarter.

Why did you give it to me anyway?

I wanted your opinion. This is your world and I'm new to it.

I'm a blip on the radar.

A big blip. You showcase some major art.

Thank you.

You're welcome; now why the delay? Give it to me straight.

No chaser?

To the head like five tequila shots.

It's a masterpiece and I cannot show it nor part with it.

Wha-What?

I'm serious. Make something else but this is mine.

You.....you can't just steal my creation, Julius!

I'm not stealing it. I'll write you a check right now.

A check? Do people still write checks?

You'll want a check. How does ten thousand sound?

Holy shit! Are you for real right now?

Real as the weather and baby, this piece is hot!

Wow. I don't know what to say.

You'll say you bank at B of A or Chase Manhattan.

What if you display it with the price and a sold tag?

I'm sorry, Jerry. As I mentioned, I cannot part with it.

I'm confused.

You've accomplished what you set out to do. You sold your art.

But no one else got to see it. What if I get a larger offer?

I'm writing the check right now.

Ten thousand, huh?

Yes. Four zeros. Your next piece may equal five.

Write the check. .

SPA DAY

Girl, this is everything. I needed this.

Like the Snickers commercial.

Right. I haven't been myself lately.

These folks are amazing. So attentive.

We could've done it big and flown to Palm Springs.

Girrrl, that spa in Palm Springs knows what they are doing.

Carl would've had a fit. He's already trippin on nothingness.

Oh, Lawd. What'd he do?

Tuesday, my fortune cookie that said I'd had a secret admirer.

Really? Who is it?

Please. I laughed so hard he got more pissed.

Oh, so he took it as book, scripture, and verse.

Asking me questions all because of a fortune cookie.

I'm sorry that is funny.

I thought he was joking but he wouldn't leave it be.

I didn't think he was insecure like that.

Me neither but he was really upset.

Take a sip of your mimosa and forget about it.

I thought I'd share before the day got away from us.

You can tell your big sis anything.

I don't know, soror, it's just not the same as before.

Do you think he's cheating on you?

He doesn't go anywhere to cheat.

You've got the internet, don't you?

Ew. No one's been in my house; that's for sure.

So what's his issue?

He's not talking to me like he used to.

Are you talking to him?

I try but he rolls his eyes out loud when I leave him alone.

I wonder what his fortune cookie said?

Hmmm.

{IS}SHOES

Wait! Uncle Bo! Uncle Bo! Wait a minute, please!

Hurry up!

Whew! You climb these Berkley hills like escalators.

Whatever. I'm ready to go.

Yeah, I guess you're mad.

Mad ain't the word. I'm pissed.

What did you expect?

I expect to be informed in advance so I can prepare.

Prepare for what? To be pissed off?

I just don't like surprises. Not like this.

Surprises? Uncle Bo, they've been together for four years.

If you gon' side with them, carry your ass back down the hill.

I rode with you Uncle Bo. You can't drive at night.

I drive just fine. I'll take the streets.

Let's go back in, Uncle Bo.

I ain't.

Allie was upset and a little embarrassed you left as you did.

She's grown especially now that she's engaged.

You can't do this, Uncle Bo.

Gimme one reason why I shouldn't just leave?

She's your daughter and she's going to need you.

For what?

To walk her down the aisle, Uncle Bo! Don't be an ass.

What your tongue, young lady. Damn XYZrs say anything.

Sorry, Uncle Bo. Excuse me.

How come you didn't say anything on the way up here?

Allie said she had a surprise for all of us. I'm elated for her.

Yeah, you squealed like a pig.

And you charged outta there like a bull so now what?

I need to think.

You do that. Take your time but do not leave!

I'mma smoke a joint and I'll be in there after I'm relaxed.

EXASPERATION

I'm headed out to get a turkey burger. Do you want anything?

Meh.

Is that 'meh' with cheese, fries, and a shake or just fries?

Very funny.

Thanks. Seriously, do you want me to grab you something?

Yes, a new job with more money, fries, and extra pickles

I don't think Tony's Deli has that but I'll check when I get there.

How can I make it stop?

Make what stop?

All this crap I have to deal with? It's like groundhog day.

Do a shitty job and get fired.

No. That's horrible. How do you combat this madness?

I think about Tony's burgers and his big smile when I show up.

That's why you work here?

No. I'm glad I'm not making burgers all day.

You do realize Tony has three locations in the city, right?

I know. And that rosy, red Porsche is his too.

So you want to be an entrepreneur now?

Not at all. I like what I do.

You are fricking confusing me, dude.

But you're not mad about your job anymore, are you?

Once you leave, I'm going to look at my screen and scream.

Here, look at this video.

OK! Oh. Oh, no! For chrissakes, what the hell is that?

The person who probably has the worst job in the world.

That's disgusting. Why do you even have that?

It reminds me this job ain't so bad and I count my blessings.

I can't imagine. Ugh. Oh my goodness. I lost my appetite.

So no burger?

I'll pass and I'm getting back to work.

DESTINATION

If I'm going to do it, I'm going to do it now.

What if you want to do it with someone special later?

I'm not waiting for a partner or a significant other.

This is a long list, Nina.

And?

Nothing. I just want you to be safe.

I have a guide and a sponsor at each destination.

I'm a little jelly but I'm happy for you.

You can meet me at any location. You have my itinerary.

Maybe when you're in Greece or Ghana.

Ghana might be a scratch. I want to do Morocco instead.

I heard it's beautiful there.

Yeah, I'm on the fence about seeing the pyramids though.

Go that far and not? How long have you been planning this?

After Robert decided to disrespect me right in front of my face.

I don't know Nina, that woman approached all of us.

You're still taking his side.

Not taking sides. She asked all of us for directions.

Mr-Help-a-Ho-Out eye-fucked her like I wasn't standing there.

Men are men, Nina. We all saw her titties out.

I didn't like it and he knew it so he got cut.

So is this trip about getting over him or something else?

I'm not waiting on anyone anymore to do what I want to do.

Plan on getting your groove back on this trip?

Me and Mr. pocket rocket will be fine.

Maybe I'll meet you in Hawaii. That's a shorter flight.

How bout Barbados?

Meh, I was there for a wedding five years ago.

A lot can change in five years

Yeah, I know but I wanna see something new, like you.

HAM-BURGULAR

Dammit!

What happened?

Someone jacked my lunch....AGAIN!

No way.

Yes, way! This is the third time this month!

Whoa. That's messed up, man.

It is more than messed up. It's petty theft.

You should report it.

I just might. This is ridiculous. Three times, man!

I have an idea.

Is it going to catch the food bandit?

It might. Kinda.

Kinda? Man, I need assurance or something.

Lace your food with a major dose of laxative.

Does that even work?

You'll find out when someone's in the bathroom a lot.

I'm not going to be a bathroom monitor.

Bet they won't mess with your food if you do it a few times.

And I still won't have lunch to eat.

I put my food in the fridge by Curt's office.

Why do you go way over there?

First, no one is going to go that far to steal food.

They might but what's the second?

I put Curt's name on it. Noone's messing with the VP's food.

Facts.

Brilliant if I may say so myself.

So what if Curt goes in there and sees his name?

Then I know Curt jacked my lunch

That's funny. Has he ever done that?

No, dude, he has a fridge in his office.

Now that is brilliant.

If I say so myself; it is.

APPETITE

It is a delight to finally see your exquisiteness in person.

And you look nothing like your profile pic.

My apologies. I don't take a lot of pictures..

It's not a bad thing. You look like you're aging backwards.

I receive that as a compliment.

It is. Your energy seemed off in the picture though.

How so?

Call me crazy but you kinda look like a different person.

Not crazy but, in my line of business, I don't take photographs.

What kind of work did you say you did?

I didn't.

So what do you do?

Recycling and Replenishing so to speak.

Recycling business too busy where you couldn't do a selfie?

What is important is that I'm here in person with you now.

I feel so lucky

You look radiant in that dress. You have a lovely neckline.

My neckline? Wow! That's different. What's your story?

I travel a great deal.

I didn't know recycling was a thing. Anywhere exciting?

I've been to places most people only dream about.

Mr. World traveler. And none of those places have women?

Elegant women have existed since the beginning of time.

Romantic. Like you saw women in the 1800s or something.

If you only knew.

Cute; a little weird but I'm getting hungry.

I thirst as well.

Wanna order some appetizers?

I am not particularly a fan of garlic.

Allergies?

Extreme.

Maybe if you bless it like this: Father, Son, Ho

Stop! I think we are done here.

What? What are you talking about?

Your Christian scheme and tempting me to eat garlic!

I never mentioned garlic, you did. You're right, we're good here.

LITTER COPS

John Bryan?

Who wants to know?

Are you Mr. Bryan?

Yeah, man, what's up?

Mr. Bryan. You've been served.

What the hell is this?

It's a citation.

A what?

At 1900 hours, you threw a bookstore receipt out your window.

What? I wasn't even in town at 19 hours; whatever you said.

Then you tossed a green apple core out the window.

How? How do you know all of this?

We're working on a highly sophisticated tracking traffic team.

It's an invasion of privacy.

You're driving in public domain, Mr. Bryan.

So y'all trash cops or something?

Something like that.

This ain't real.

It's very real, Mr. Bryan.

First the red light camera,

Now the Pollution Patrol

TIME TO GO

Yo, where's Nate? I thought he was coming.

Nate isn't living his best life right now.

Oh, God. Did something happen with him and Patty?

Yep. Broke up. Kicked him out and he's at his mom's.

Damn.

Worse. Karl saw him at the back of McDonald's at closing.

No! No Way!

No cap. Karl circled back to find out if he was OK.

He had to be at a low point to intercept food before its trash.

Karl said his throat was too emotional to talk to him.

Wow. I knew stuff was raggedy with them but not this bad.

I'm certain Patty gave him umpteen times to strikeout.

But to kick your man out and he's pilfering at Mickie D's?

And staying with his moms.

I could never go back home.

Or could you?

I wouldn't let it get to that point.

You never know a person until you need to know them.

Nate's got a great network of friends, contacts, and colleagues.

Pinching the bridge of your nose won't fix this.

I'm trying to think. Who can we call?

Karl said Nate said not to help him. He wants to work it out.

But he's at his mom's house. That's the ultimate low.

A mother's love is never low, dude.

That's not what I meant.

I know.

Shit!

What?

Nate's birthday is in two days.

Let's go get him.

HWY 9 - PART 1

You got some nerve showing up here unannounced.

It's an emergency. Have you heard from Cassie?

Not yet. Supposed to be driving back home for break.

Something's wrong.

Ain't nothing wrong.

I had a few missed calls from her but they were one ring.

What's that floozy in the car have to do with it?

She's my partner, Alyce. We're investigating a crime.

Did you call her back?

Several times. Her mailbox is full.

Maybe she's in a bad connection area. She'll call back.

Will you call me if she calls you?

No.

This isn't about us. I want to make sure she's OK.

If she calls, I'll tell her to call you.

Thank you.

But I ain't calling you.

Got it. You made that clear.

And don't be rolling up here unannounced with your bitch.

She's my partner. We're on our way to a crime scene.

Whatever.

If you answered your phone, I would not have shown up.

Whatever.

Let me know if Cassie calls. Please.

As I said, I'll tell her to call you.

Thank you.

HWY 9 - PART 2

Dad?

Cass. Thank God! Where are you, Sweetie?

Highway 9. I'm about 90 minutes out, maybe? Wuzzup?

I'm glad you called me back. Are you OK?

Yep. Just stopped for gas and brought a new charger.

Good. Call your mom and let her know you're safe, please.

OK. About that.

What's up?

Can I stay at your place during my break?

Sure. I'm sure she's expecting you but, is everything OK?

We can talk about it when I see you.

Of course.

If it's an issue, I'll go to Cousin Shelly or Tammy's house.

Don't be silly, baby. My house is your house. Still have a key?

Mmmhmm.

Cool. Call your mom and let her know your plans.

I'll text her. She won't care.

What's up with you two?

She's just been different after you two split up.

Different how?

I dunno. Angry all the time. Leaving me weird messages.

Weird like what?

One of them was like, 'you think you're better than me.'

Yeah, that's different even for your mom.

Exactly. I think she does it in her sleep or something.

Is she drinking again?

A lot more than before.

We'll talk more when you're home. Call me when you arrive.

Will do.

Love you.

Love you too, Daddy and thanks.

Anytime.

HWY 9 - PART 3

Your ex is a piece of work, partner.

I know how to pick 'em.

Don't be so hard on yourself. We learn from our past.

So we can have a better future?

That's the quest.

How's your sitcho with Reid?

Has insecurities about dating, and I quote, "law enforcement."

Is that why he moved?

He accepted a transfer which gave him an easy excuse.

But are you still trying to, you know, make it work?

Reid knew who I was and what I did when we met.

I figured. You're a straight shooter, no pun intended.

Right. He thought female cops were sexy.

So what happened?

Bad cops doing bad shit everywhere. Breanna Taylor for sure.

Why that situation?

He's from Louisville.

We're far from Kentucky.

He lumps all of us as part of the problem.

They don't see the good shit; only what's on the news.

And that's 100% bad stuff.

Reid's an idiot with all due respect.

Your ex too. Alyce, right?

Yep; we married when we were young and dumb.

I thought she was gonna fire lasers from her eyes.

Don't take it personally. She's always been like that.

Ah, the jealous type. What did you do?

She lets her mind tell her things that aren't true.

Shame.

Cassie was the only good thing we created together.

I hope she gets home safe.

HWY 9 - PART 4

Jesus! What do you want?

Is Cassandra here?

No. She's on her way back from school. I told my ex that.

Can you step outside to talk, please? I can come in if you like.

Hell no. This is my house. Tell my ex-husband that.

This is a police matter, Alyce.

So he sends his bitch to do his police work for him, huh?

Your daughter phoned her father from Highway 9 at 2pm.

And? What's that got to do with me?

The vehicle security chip pinged at 2:27. It brought us here.

Maybe she arrived and went for a walk. I dunno.

Alyce?

What, bitch? What are you pointing at?

Is that your daughter's Camry?

Yeah, but she ain't here. I just told you that.

I need to come inside.

Need a warrant for that, dumb-dumb.

It would be easier for you and David if we all talked about this.

Are you fucking David?

No ma'am. We're trying to locate your daughter.

Uh-huh. You're fucking him. I know his type.

Cass has not contacted you or indicated she was home?

Y'all doing it doggy-style or are you on top?

Here's my card. Please call me if your daughter contacts you.

Whatever.

Please, Alyce. It's your daughter.

I know.

We see terrible things on this job. We want her home safely.

She'll be alright. She's independent just like her momma.

HWY 9 - PART 5

My head is throbbing. Where could she be?

You should go home in case she shows up.

Good idea. She said she wasn't going to her mother's house.

What's interesting, Dave. She said she was 90 minutes away.

Right and the location device already had her car in the city.

I wonder if we can trace her last call's location?

It wouldn't hurt to try.

If she and her mom aren't jelling, why drop the car there?

Whatever their beef is, that was Cass' chess move.

You think.

Alyce bought a Benz with the alimony settlement.

She's the real deal.

Alyce gave Cass the Camry before she left for college.

As a gift?

Cass saw right through it.

Regardless; how come she hasn't called you?

Not sure.

You've got that scowl when you have a hunch.

Just a tingling feeling.

Spill it, Spiderman.

Cass was on Highway 9 when she called me.

Right; from a gas station, yes. What about it?

Only two gas stations, maybe, on Highway 9.

I'll make some calls.

Copy.

I better let Roy know what's happening.

Roy's looped in. I called after my chat with Alyce.

Appreciate ya, partner.

I got your back. We've got eyes on Alyce's house too.

Perfect.

HWY 9 – PART 6

Heard from Cass yet?

Nothing yet. I'm trying not to get worried but it's too late.

Do you remember Burt Jackson? We used to call him Big Burt?

Big Burt? Of course, what's up with him? How's retired life?

He's the Sherriff of Teal County and….

Highway 9 runs through Teal. Damn, I have a great partner.

Thank me after we locate Cassie.

Deal. What is Burt talking about? Anything at the gas stations?

More than he signed up for. Like some Area 51 stuff.

Huh?

Surveillance cameras at the gas station don't capture any cars.

Are they not positioned to record the cars?

That's the thing. All the cameras are by the pumps and doors.

Jeez; that's weird for sure.

The recording shows people walking in and out but…..

But?

Once they get to their cars, nothing.

Did Burt check it out?

Of course, he did. The clerk verified people got gas and food.

How long has this been going on?

Three nights ago. Clerk called Burt about a drunk customer.

What happened?

Burt took him to the precinct and somebody picked him up.

How'd he get to the gas station?

He drove.

But no visibility of the car from the cams?

Nope.

Strange.

Clerk said he became intemperate over breaking a 100.

We gotta go see Big Burt.

I set up a Zoom call. You have to stay put for Cassie.

You are awesome.

HWY 9 - PART 7

Big Burt! How's life in Teal County?

If I knew retirement was this busy I'd be back in the city.

Hey, you said you were tired of the fast life.

I wouldn't trade this for anything. Mostly 201s or speeding.

Where are people disorderly in Teal County?

Bar and grill out here. You can't see it from the highway.

Locals?

Mostly but the college kids know about it too.

Speaking of college kids. Did the clerk see my daughter?

Yeah. Bought some coconut water, a charger, and a candy bar.

But nothing outside?

Just like all the other customers. Once they're outside, nothing.

Strange.

You're telling me. I spent 800 bucks on replacing those cams.

Same result?

Yeah. I feel like I wasted the department's budget.

Repurpose the old ones since they still work.

Good idea. Any word from your daughter?

Nothing yet. Seems like she was in the city when she called.

She'll turn up. These kids are so independent nowadays.

My ex said the same thing.

Yikes. How's that going - ya know - the divorce?

Happier than ever.

Well, you're looking good. Did you lose some weight?

I actually get up early and run a couple of miles every day.

On purpose?

Yeah, wiseass. I'm not semi-retired like you.

Well, I'm bout ready to shut it down and move to Tampa.

Too many mosquitoes.

Better than the weirdos in Teal County.

HWY 9 - PART 8

Hey partner. How'd the chat with Burt go?

She was in the store but nothing after that.

The timestamp of her call and the ping from the car don't match.

That's a head-scratcher.

Do you think we put missing persons on it?

We're right about at that time frame.

I hope she's at a boy's house.

Oh, you do?

Not like that, dude. Hanging out, ya know?

I guess it's time to call Alyce and find out.

But Cass said they weren't talking much.

Maybe it's because of a boy.

You know how mothers are with their daughters.

I thought it was the opposite?

No way. I was a complete Daddy's girl.

I can see that. Maybe Reid saw that too.

He didn't wanna see *my* Daddy.

No guy wants to see their girl's pops.

So what are we doing?

I'm sending Alyce a text.

I'll call Chuck in Missing Persons.

Here we go.

HWY 9 - PART 9

Hi Daddy!

Cass! Oh my goodness. Where are you?

On Highway 9. I'm about 45 minutes away from home.

Highway 9? Did you turn around and go back for something?

Go back? No, but I picked up a car charger at a gas station.

You told me that already. Yesterday, remember?

Huh? This is my first time calling you. I left you a message.

Cass, You called me. You asked if you could stay with me.

Stay with you?

Yes, during your break.

Uh, I don't remember asking you that.

You did. You said something about you and your mom.

I am so confused right now. What about mom?

Your car is at your mother's house. Right now.

Well, that's not possible if I'm driving. Are you OK, Daddy?

Stay on the phone with me while I drive to your mother's.

She'll be thrilled to see you now that she's sober.

Wait. What? Yesterday, you said she was drinking.

Mom? Yeah, drinking Perrier with lemon.

This is making my nose hair burn.

Weird. Are you sure you're OK?

Cass, I'm pulling up to your mother's house now.

That was quick.

Seems like other patrol cars are here too.

What's up with that?

Not sure. Crime scene unit is here too.

WOW, the block is hot. Nothing happens in our neighborhood.

I'll find out in a second. Hold on.

HWY 9 – PART 10

Dave! Hey, partner, I've been trying to reach you.

What's going on here? I got Cass on the line.

What? How, how is she on the line?

I'm talking to her. I've been on with her for about 15 minutes.

Dave, we need to talk for a minute before you go over there.

Hold on. Cass? Cass. Cass!

Dave!

What? Why isn't she responding? Cass?

Dave!

What, goddammit?

Cass is….I dunno how to say this, It's not pretty, partner.

What?

We found her body, Dave. I'm….I'm so, so sorry.

This is insane. Cass just said she was driving home.

Alyce is in custody. We're taking her to the station now.

What the fuck are you talking about?

Alyce, Dave. We're taking her in for questioning.

Cass is on the line with me now. Here, talk to her.

No, Dave.

She's on the line! Here, talk to her. Cass, answer me!

She's gone, Dave.

No! Listen, she's on the line! She's on the line!

"Hi, Daddy. I'm home now. Everything's going to be alright. I'm here with Nana and Grandpa Lou. It's beautiful here. I love you."

IMPATIENCE

911 What's your emergency?

Uh, I don't have one but it's an emergency.

What is the emergency, sir?

I just came home from work and -

Has your home been burglarized, sir?

No. My place is fine, I parked my car and saw -

Is there a fire or an emergency in your neighborhood, sir?

No. Listen to me! I came home and saw a man on a bench.

What is your address, sir?

My address? The man is outside of my apartment.

Which apartment, sir?

Maple Leaf Apartment Complex.

Dangerous area.

I live on the north side.

We get calls from the north side too.

Never had issues on this side.

What is the emergency with the man on the bench, sir?

Yeah, right; he followed me and knocked on my door.

Did he attempt to break in?

No, please, let me finish.

Go on.

I answered and he asked could he use my phone.

OK.

I wasn't comfortable letting him in because he could rob me.

Understood. Is he still outside your door?

No, I told him I'd call 911 for him.

What is *his* emergency?

He's been stabbed or shot.

Don't you think you should have led your call with this?

I didn't notice it until I saw a pool of blood by the steps.

You could have stated someone has been stabbed.

I was trying to.

UNTIMELY DISCRETION

Say it with me, 'nothing happened.'

I'm not saying that.

If you don't say it, it won't be true.

How do I say nothing happened when it did?

Like that. You say it the way you said it.

I don't even believe it. I don't think its believable.

You don't have to; you just have to say it convincingly.

How about, 'it was an accident?'

A red-light runner hitting another car is an accident.

No, that's a crash.

Well, what we did was certainly no accident.

It was an accident. It wasn't supposed to happen.

And that's why you say, "nothing happened."'

And I'm supposed to tell Allen that?

No. Hell No. You're not telling anyone except yourself.

Huh?

What's the smug on your face for? Just say it.

It just happened, I mean, nothing happened

Say it again.

Nothing happened. Christ! Nothing happened. Satisfied?

See? Its easy. It is what it is.

He's going to know as soon as he sees me.

What is he going to know?

That something happened.

Nothing happened.

Easy for you to say. Cheryl is oblivious to your shit.

Ouch.. Something happened, but it was seven years ago.

That doesn't help either.

We can't stay back here too long so what's the gameplan?

Nothing happened. Nothing happened. Satisfied?

Sure, if you are. Now introduce me to your husband.

TRUST YOUR GUT

Yo! Craziest shit just happened.

Where you at? Sounds like a party or something.

Nah, I had to step out at Jake's Pub to have a brew or two.

Whoa, what the heck happened?

The new SVP invites me and Vee over for drinks.

OK, good stuff. Networking with the honcho. He's new, right?

Apparently not that new. He and Vee know each other.

Word?

Yeah, I thnk that ninja smashed my wife.

Oh, hell nah, man. Get the heck outta here.

I know what I saw and they looked too familiar with each other.

Whatchu sayin?

I'm saying they'd shared a familiar look about them.

Huh?

You know that look, man, come on!

Every man knows the look. What did Vee say in the car?

Said he used to kick it with a friend, Treneeka, in college.

You don't believe her?

Hell nah, I don't believe her. Shit sounded made up from jump.

Come on, bro, its likely dude knew your wife but not smash.

That ninja bit his bottom lip and we know what that shit means.

Oh, shit, man. I'm sorry.

You're sorry. I gotta work with this SOB everyday.

Whatchu drinkin, I'm on my way.

Yeah, hurry up before I'm drunk, divorced, fired and arrested.

CHANGE THE GAME

This is my public service announcement that I'm doing me.

Congratulations.

Nah, man, you don't get it. I'm serious. I'm disappearing.

You're accepted no matter what you do - without judgement.

I'm breaking away and getting new friends.

You're on one, bro. What will you do with your old friends?

They'll still exist but I'm freeing myself.

Big gamble. Where did this revelation come from?

The last party I had. You were there.

It was probably one of the dopest events I've been to.

Do you remember seeing me there?

I remember seeing you - mingling with the ladies.

Wrong. They wanted to know who was the owner of the house.

I'm assuming you told them.

Pffft. And ruin the suspense? They thought it was an AirBnB.

I think I get it. You didn't know them and vice versa?

Someone brought them or told them about MY event.

Yet, noone introduced you and they had no clue who you were.

Its disrespectful.

Maybe the person wasn't timely with their intros.

Its the principle.Someone brought strangers to my house.

People bring a plus-one to an event all the time.

A real friend would have extended a proper introduction.

Consider the circumstances. Your parties are epic.

And all those invited normally find the host.

So you're inviting a new subset of people next time?

I'm doing something different.

I'mma pray for you that you come out better with this new plan.

Its already in motion. Salaam.

THIS IS WHAT WE'RE DOING?

Owen Jones.

In the flesh. This is what what doing? Government names?

You couldn't call, text or email when you were coming to town?

I, listen.

I randomly see you at the mall with this cute darling. Who is this?

This. This is my daughter, April.

Well, hello, April with your cute self. You must look like your mother.

Very funny.

No laughing matter.

No one's laughing, right?

What are you doing here? They don't have malls in Omaha?

I'm here for William's installation.

Well you couldn't miss that could you. Of all things . . .

He's my best friend and after Madison passed - -

Oh, save the theatrics and excuses. You could have called.

I was going to. We left April's shoes in Philly and - -

So Bruce knew your were here and didn't call me? Wonderful!

I told him not to. I wanted to surprise you.

You're full of surprises and something else, right, April?

I promise. We stopped to get April some shoes and - -

And then call me?

Yes, and, and invite you to dinner to meet April and June.

Lemme guess, is there another kid named May?

Clever, but no.

Aren't you too old to be procreating?

Let's meet for dinner. I'll call you once we're settled.

Does the Ritz still hold a room for you on the fifth floor?

Yes.

I'll see you and I'll see you too, little April Sunshine. Cutesy.

Can I get a hug or something?

Why not.

It was a pleasure seeing you.

Yeah, you too, Dad. See you at dinner.

WHO KNEW [SUBJECT TO CHANGE]

When I agreed to this party, I thought we'd be on time.

You know you cannot rush a woman.

You're right. Look at the clock and add 51 minutes.

Hush. I'm ready.

Are you?

Which earrings should I wear?

The ones that go in your ears.

I'm serious.

Me too. Don't get me caught in your wardrobe trap.

Excuse me.

You never like my suggestions or recommendations.

I wouldn't be asking you.

I thought you said you were ready.

I am.

Those.

Excuse me?

The earrings in your right hand. Wear those.

The hoops will look better, but thanks.

See? That's why I don't - -

I was just kidding, I'm going to wear the ones you picked.

Now can we go?

One sec, I'm sending Kya a text.

Because?

She asked me what I was wearing.

She what?

She was debating on wearing a dress we picked out together.

On our trip? That was three years ago.

We just dont want to wear the same thing.

I'm not going to say it, but I know you know what I'm thinking.

Hush.

WRONG SIDE OF THE TRACKS

Hey, young man. What are you doing over there?

Nothing.

You don't belong around here.

I'm just playing.

Its not safe to play around here. You can get hurt.

I'm being careful.

Who you kin to?

Excuse me?

I said, who you kin to? Where your people stay?

I don't live here. I'm visiting my grandparents for the summer.

Who your peoples, son?

My pop-pop is Fred Rooney.

Fred Rooney, huh? He ain't gonna like you being over here.

I'm just playing.

Train tracks ain' no place for a kid to play, youngin..

You talk funny.

That's neither here nor there. You best get home, son.

How come?

You don't question your elders, you hear me?

Yes but you don't have to yell.

This is ain't no place for someone your age.

I'm 10 years old.

All the while. Do I need to call your grandfather?

No. No ma'am.

As I said, this ain't no place for a 10-year-old playing.

OK

Mind your manners, young man.

OK.

Bad things happenin' here. I'd hate for it to happen to you.

Like what?

Like little boys like you not making it home to their pah-pah.

If you're trying to scare me, its working.

Good. Now get gone.

Wha?

I'm telling you to get yourself back to your peoples. Now!

I'm leaving.

Right now.

Yes, ma'am. Right now

CRIMINAL MINDED

I'm glad you came through.

I didn't say I was going to do it.

Come on, man, we need you.

I'm not sure about this.

I've worked it out, man. Its practically fail safe.

What's the next move?

We make copies of the keys at the hardware store.

Talk about an obvious way to get caught.

Nah, man, they have do-it-yourself machines in there.

So we make copies. What if the whips aren't there?

They'll be there. They're always there. I've been on this.

And if they ain't?

We wait.

OK, I thought you said you were on a time crunch.

My people know this is a major job so they'll wait for us.

Hmmm.

Come on, man, don't punk out; we need six drivers.

You need six drivers not me.

You know the route.

Who doesn't? Straight up the parkway.

Right. Its a no-brainer.

Its too obvious, fam.

Where's all this hesitancy all of a sudden? What's good?

I took a run up the parkway last Tuesday and Friday.

Good stuff.

Not exactly. Troopers are laced up and down the reststops.

Man, they just getting donuts and chillin.

I dunno.

We'll do the speed limit.

First, no one does the speedlimit on the parkway.

Then we'll speed.

Listen to yourself.

We gotta get this done, yo. There's a lot of bread involved.

Its risky.

Scared money don't make none.

Answer this correctly and I'll make your deision.

Why are your trippin? What's your question? I'm getting pissed.

Six Dodge Chargers riding up the parkway don't seem weird?

Man, there's plenty of Chargers up and down the parkway.

Pfffft.

Smack your lips all you want, bro. We're doing this!

It don't feel right.

Think of the dough we're about to get.

I'm thinking about it. Your guy's good for it?

I've been doing jobs like this since I was 13.

Times have changed since your days out North-West.

Trussme, we good!

Don't these whips have fobs?

Not these models. I've covered all the tracks.

Hmmm.

Look, you're in too deep. You gotta rock wth us now.

Or?

I'll be forced to get big Hal involved and I don't wanna do that.

Wow; turning me over to your goons?

We all have our vices, man, so lets get this money.

I'm one and done with this shit, man.

I'm glad you've chosen the right path, my good brother.

It doesnt feel like I have a choice.

POPPA KNOWS

Well, isn't this a surprise?

Do you still cook fish on Friday?

You know I do.

Then you shouldn't be surprised.

I figured you forgot.

Why is that?

I haven't seen you in a month of Sundays.

Not a month.

Where have you been?

I've been driving to Virginia after work every Thursday.

Is that so? You don't work on Fridays anymore?

I do two 12-hour shifts Tuesday and Wednesday.

Impressive.

Thank ya!

Whatever or *WHOever* is in Virginia must be worth it.

All facts!

Don't burn yourself out.

I don't know, Pops. I'm doing all the work to make it work.

The Bible says, *Hard work always pays off; mere talk puts no bread on the table.*

Is that in the Bible for real?

Are you questioning your father?

Ha, no, sir, and you can put the knife down.

Theresa is a nice girl.

Appreciate that, Pops.

I've always liked her over that nasty Niecy.

Really, Pops?

No respect for elders.

Dang, Pops, don't hold back, why don't yoa?

Your mother wasn't ever impressed.

I know, Dad. It was a thing, and Niecy is no more.

Good.

I'm really feeling Teri, but…

But?

A part of me wants her to move on without me; do her thing.

I don't understand.

I drive down to Virginia to spend time with her and see how she's doing without me.

Well, if you're going down there every weekend and spending three or four days, she can't miss you.

What do you mean?

Absence makes the heart grow fonder. Skip a weekend.

That's what I'm doing, and having fish on Friday with Pops

MmmHmm.

I'm serious, plus I wanted to get your advice about Teri.

Ain't none of my business with you young people. Worse than those reality shows your mother watches.

Wait, I thought you liked Teri.

Theresa landed a great job down there, and you think she will forget about you like that?

What's with the knife? Put that down. What are you saying?

All she did was move out of state. She didn't stop caring about you. Otherwise, she'd tell you to stop wasting your gas driving to see her.

That's true.

"He who findeth a wife finds a good thing and earns favor from the Lord."

Wife? I didn't say anything about no wife.

You might as well be with all this thinking, worrying, and traveling. Do you love her?

Come on, dad, you know I do.

Then do the right thing and stop playing. It's probably why she took the job in Virginia in the first place.

Huh?

She wants you to prove that you want her in your life.

Driving down every week doesn't show that?

Have you told her how you feel?

About driving down to Virginia? No.

Please don't make me throw this fish grease on you.

I assumed we felt the same way and didn't have to discuss it.

Communication is vital in every relationship, especially a long-distance one.

"Let us not love with words or speech but with actions and in truth, for your actions speak louder than your words."

That's my boy.

Now, wuzzup with that catfish, Pops?

Come and get it.

WHAT HAD HAPPENED

Hello?

Cool Curt, wuzzup, my brotha?

Danny-O, same ole, same ole. What's good in your hood?

I'm actually in yo city, Doc.

Right on. How long are you town, my man?

I just touched down for three days - work stuff, ya know?

Nice. We gotta get together. Where are your staying?

I'm at this hotel near the airport.

Lots of hotels by the airport, cuzzin. Which one?

Don't matter. They won't let me check in for another four hours.

Four hours?

Yeah, man, come scoop me so we can grab a bite.

Right now?

NO! Next Tuesday. Of course, right now so these folk stop looking at me.

Bruh, I can't break out for at least another hour.

Damn. An hour?

Yeah, sixty minutes. You can Uber out to me.

I don't like Uber.

OK. How about Lyft?

I'm kinda banned from Lyft.

I don't wanna know, do I?

Nah, you dont.

What hotel has you waiting for four hours?

I'm booked at the City Suites but they won't take my card.

Your corporate card?

Yeah. I guess I'm flagged by them off some BS in Chicago.

Chicago? You love that city.

And the city loves me back but not the City Suites.

Do I want to know?

Man, I don't even know. Chicago is a blur.

EDUTAINMENT

Now that was interesting.

You can say that again.

Did you like the movie?

It was cool but,

You didn't like it.

I said it was cool.

Which means there was something about it you didn't like.

The movie was a'ight.

But?

I just don't like how we're depicted in every friggin' movie.

Oh, I feel you. We're always the antagonist.

We're always the bad guys.

Yes, the nemesis, the foe, also known as the bad guy.

Yes, smarty, all of that.

Or the junkie, the drug dealer, the servant.

Don't forget the rebellious one who dies first.

That part.

Every movie can't be Wakanda though.

I get that, and I'm not expecting that. I don't think I would watch Wakanda every Friday, but

But?

Hidden agendas, themes, and symbols are snuck into movies.

Psychological easter eggs in every movie impact our minds.

True. Animated movies are the worst for that.

No doubt.

And we let our babies watch them without us.

We need righteous movies.

Someone still has to move the hero to the next level.

You're suggesting conflict resolution or something.

We have to know how they will get out of the mess or drama.

But *we* don't have to be the conflict or the adversary.

You must remember who's telling these stories.

Well, *we* need more storytellers.

We have them. What we need is the key to the gates.

Or another path.

There's always an unchartered path.

That's the path that will free us.

Mainstream isn't the only stream.

Oooh, you're getting deep on a brother.

It's also capitalism at work.

So I guess it's fair to say we didn't like this movie?

No.